P·A·Y·O·F·F
FOR THE BANKER

Books by Frances and Richard Lockridge

Dead as a Dinosaur

Death Takes a Bow

Death of a Tall Man

The Dishonest Murderer

Hanged for a Sheep

Killing the Goose

Murder Is Served

Murder Out of Turn

Murder Within Murder

The Norths Meet Murder

Payoff for the Banker

A Pinch of Poison

P·A·Y·O·F·F
FOR THE BANKER

FRANCES & RICHARD
LOCKRIDGE

HarperPerennial
A Division of HarperCollins*Publishers*

Originally published in hardcover in 1945 by J. B. Lippincott Company.

HarperCollins books may be purchased for educational, business, or sales promotional use. For information please write: Special Markets Department, Harper-Collins Publishers, Inc., 10 East 53rd Street, New York, NY 10022.

First HarperPerennial edition published 1994.

Designed by R. Caitlin Daniels

Library of Congress Cataloging-in-Publication Data

Lockridge, Frances Louise Davis.
    Payoff for the banker / by Frances and Richard Lockridge. — 1st HarperPerennial ed.
        p. cm.
    ISBN 0-06-092514-0
    1. North, Jerry (Fictitious character)—Fiction. 2. North, Pam (Fictitious character)—Fiction. 3. Private investigators—New York (N.Y.)—Fiction. 4. Women detectives—New York (N.Y.)—Fiction.
I. Lockridge, Richard, 1898–   . II. Title.
PS3523.O243D434 1994
813' .54—dc20   93-40505

94 95 96 97 98 ❖/CW 10 9 8 7 6 5 4 3 2 1

P·A·Y·O·F·F
FOR THE BANKER

• 1 •

TUESDAY, JUNE 13, 5:40 P.M. TO 6:05 P.M.

For the first time in more than a year—in fourteen months and some days and some hours—she felt young, as if things were beginning over. So they were right after all; the obvious was almost always right; the old saws came true. You did not believe they would—you knew they never would. Because the experiences other people had—the worn, accustomed experiences—were not the experiences you would have. And then, in the end, they were. In the end you went on living and things began over. In the end you felt young again. And after a while, she realized, she would not even be surprised that this was so.

They had told her, some of them gently because they remembered when they had believed otherwise, that it was not so hard when you were young—or that it was not so hard for so long. If she and Rick had had more time it would in the end have been harder, although that was difficult to understand. If it had worked out, of course, since otherwise the problem did not come up—it was another problem and part of the chance everyone took. If they had had even a year and then it had happened it would have been harder; if they had had five years, and it had worked out, it would have been desperately hard. And beyond that the old saws did not work, because they worked only on averages and beyond a certain number of years there were no averages. You grew together—and that almost without regard for the quality of your feelings for each other—and you were not as individuals, predictable. That, at any rate, was what they had told her, some of them.

But she and Rick had had quite a bit less than a year and it had not gone beneath excitement—a very beautiful excitement. Before there had been only the beginning of exploration and then there had been the beautiful excitement and then, as if a knife had cut, there had been nothing. Then people had told her comforting things which did not comfort and a lieutenant-commander who headed Rick's squadron had written a letter about what a great guy Rick had been and it was as if he were writing about another Rick altogether. As probably, she realized now, he was. He was writing about a Rick who had taken a Wildcat roaring off a carrier deck and she had never seen Rick fly. He was writing about a Rick who had come back toward the carrier one afternoon and circled to land and had been talked off because Zeros were following him to find the carrier and had turned away and headed out for nothing, with the Zeros turning too, and had said, "I'll be seeing you," when he knew he would never be seeing any of them again. That was Rick, but it was not really the Rick she knew. Now, after fourteen months and some days, she could not remember how his voice must have sounded as he said it. And she had never been sure. They hadn't had long enough.

So Rick was dead. She had never fooled herself about that, and nobody had tried to fool her. It had ended as if a knife had cut it. And she hadn't ended, in spite of what she thought. Now she was beginning over.

She was taking up ordinary things again. She was walking along Madison Avenue, on the shady side of the street, and she was carrying a tall paper bag. It was so tall that, as it rested in the crook of her right arm, the top of it—with the loaf of bread sticking out—was at the level of her eyes. She was coming to the corner of Madison and Seventy-third Street and waiting for the lights to cross to the sunny side because she lived on the sunny side. She was a girl who worked in an office, going home to a three-room apartment she had sublet, furnished, and taking lamb chops and other things so that she could cook herself dinner—lamb chops and salad—and eat them by herself with a book propped up against an ugly, but solid, brown vase. All the rest of it was ended, and this was another beginning. She was twenty-three and she was going home to her apartment after work with all the things, in addition to the lamb chops, that you need when a kitchen is just beginning. It was not exciting, but it was satisfying. She was not ready yet for new excitement, but now she knew that she would be ready for it—some time. There was no hurry—it was an unimmediate part of a future which might hold anything and so might hold even that. Because now a hurt was a memory.

In the future, and this realization was part of the new beginning, she might be hurt again—and might be happy again in that bright way you could be happy, so that you knew consciously you were happy. But not now, and not tomorrow and not next month—probably not next month. Tonight and tomorrow, and the days after, until Saturday and Sunday at Beth Arnold's outside Chappaqua, and through Saturday and Sunday and for another week at the office—for that time she would merely be safe and comfortable, and only little things would happen.

It was time she had weeks and months like that, Mary Hunter decided. For a girl of twenty-three there had been plenty that was not restful. Even before Rick; back when she was nineteen and had hated a man because of what he had done to her through another man. And that, of course, should have shown her that things do not last forever, even including hate and love. Because now it was absurd that she had ever hated the old boy and thought he had destroyed her. That was how she had thought of it then—that he had destroyed her. It appeared now that healthy young women were not "destroyed" at nineteen, or even at twenty-three. It was even possible that he had done her a good turn, without intending anything so benevolent.

But it had been exciting and turbulent and she had not much more than got over it when there was Rick. And now, comfortably, there was nothing but a three-room apartment, furnished, certainly, with a minimum of excitement, and two lamb chops. At their best, which she gloomily supposed hers would not be, lamb chops did not furnish much excitement. They were merely appropriate—dull without being completely enervating.

She walked up four steps and into the hall which ran along the side of the antique shop and passed the door which said: JAMES SELDEN, ANTIQUES. The old man who ran the elevator was sitting in a wooden chair propped back against the wall at the end of the corridor and he did not move until she was at the elevator door. Then he brought the chair down with a tired plunk and groaned a small, obviously conventionalized groan and stood up. His standing was an indication that the elevator was in operation, that he would consent to operate it and that Mary Hunter, widow of Lieut. (j.g.) Richard Hunter, U.S.N.R., missing and presumed dead in action in the Pacific, holder of the Distinguished Flying Cross and, posthumously, of the Navy Cross, might enter and ride.

Mary entered, balancing the tall bag of things she had bought at the delicatessen which was really a grocery, and the old man sighed.

"Four, ain't it, Miss?" he said, proving that he already knew her. And she had only rented the apartment on Sunday and had slept in it for the first time on Monday night, and now it was Tuesday and she was ready to cook in it for the first time. She smiled at him, because he, also, was appropriate to the worn peacefulness of her new life. So was the pace of the elevator, which trundled upward as if its mind were elsewhere.

It had stopped with what amounted to a sigh of relief at the fourth floor and Mary Hunter smiled at the old man, who merely looked at her, and went down the corridor to her door. *Her* door, which she could close after her. She passed the head of the narrow flight of stairs, with the metal treads of fire resistance, which offered an alternative— probably frequently necessary—to the elevator, and put the bag down in the corner by the door while she got the key out of her purse. She opened the door, pushing it away from her, and picked up the heavy bag again and went into her own hall, which was short and opened into the living room. She took three or four quick steps down the hall before she noticed.

And then she stopped and the bag fell from her arm and there was the crack of glass breaking in it and she stared into the living room.

She did not move for a moment and she did not say anything, but merely looked into the living room. And then she said, in a voice which was higher in pitch than her own, but not louder, "No. No! Not you again. Not *again!*"

And then she went on into the living room.

She did not scream. The old man in the elevator was certain that he would have heard her if she screamed, because he had waited—out of sheer inertia, so far as a motive could subsequently be ascribed—until she had entered the apartment, before he started down in the car. So he would have heard her scream, if she had screamed. She could say only that she did not know whether she had screamed or not, and that the elevator man probably was right. She had to say this a good many times, to a good many people, all of whom were certain she would have screamed if things had been the way she said they were. The argument was that since she did not scream, things were not as she said they were. This argument was advanced in words and reflected in faces.

Pamela North turned off the shower, pulled the bathing cap—which was made of plastic, apparently—off her head and discovered the telephone was ringing. It was ringing as if it had been ringing a long time. Pam North said, "Damn!" with feeling. "Alexander Graham Bell," Mrs. North said, angrily. "Damn! Or Thomas Edison, or whoever."

The telephone rang again. It was not to be vanquished.

"All *right,*" Pam said. "And when I get there you'll have gone away."

She opened the curtains and the telephone rang again. It was insistent, and Pam decided it probably was Jerry.

"He ought to know I'd be taking a bath," she said. "I always am."

The presence of Ruffy in the hall, indignant at being shut out, kept Pam North from the appearance of talking to herself. Obviously she was talking to Ruffy. Pam reached for her robe and the telephone bell interjected commandingly.

"After all," Pam said, "it's Jerry. So it's all right. I don't *need* anything on."

She went to the telephone, without anything on, and dripping. She was too wet to sit down and she had already left wet footprints from bath to living room. She lifted the telephone out of its cradle and said, "Yes, dear."

The voice was strange. It was not Jerry's voice, and it was strange for any voice.

"Pamela North?" the voice said. It was a woman's voice. "I want to speak to Pamela North, *please*."

There was urgency in the "please."

"Yes," Pamela said. "You are. This is—"

A key was in the lock and the door opened. Jerry came in and stopped just inside and looked at her. He nodded and smiled.

"Very nice, too," he said.

"Wait a minute," Pam said to the telephone. "I thought it was you, or I'd have put something on," she said. "It isn't you."

"It certainly—" Jerry said.

"On the telephone, silly," Pam said.

"—better be," Jerry finished. "Under the circumstances." He looked at her with deliberate care. "Very pretty circumstances," he added and went on toward his study.

"Mrs. North?" the voice said. "Pamela North?"

Pamela was brought back from her thoughts, which were that Jerry was very sweet, really.

"Yes," she said. "This is Pamela North. Who is this?"

"Mary Hunter," the voice said. Now that Mrs. North could give it her attention, there was no doubt that the voice was high and strained. "You've got to help me."

"All right," Pam said. "I'll help you. Mary what?"

"Hunter," the voice said. "Mrs. Richard Hunter. You've got to remember. At Billy Clarkson's a week ago Sunday."

"Oh," Pam said. "Of course. Mary Hunter. Of course I remember you."

She did remember her, vaguely. A slender, quick girl with short light hair, whose husband had been a Navy flyer and had been killed. A girl who just seemed to be coming out of it.

"Yes, Mary," Pam repeated. "Of course—and I'd love to—to help you. If I can."

"He's dead," the voice of Mary Hunter said. "I know he's dead—there's—there's blood all over. Just lying there. When I came home."

"I don't—" Pam began.

"I found him," the voice said. And now it sounded as if it would break at any moment. "And I don't know what to do. And you and Mr. North know the police and—"

"Yes," Pam said. "You mean you found a body? The body of somebody who has been killed? In your apartment?"

"Yes," Mary Hunter said. "Yes. Oh, God—yes!"

"Do you know—it?" Mrs. North said.

There was a little pause, and Pamela could hear the girl breathing—quickly, desperately.

"It's—it's the old boy," she said. "Josh's father. So you've got to help me. I'm—I'm afraid."

"Have you called the police?" Pam said.

The girl hadn't.

"Just you," she said. "I've—I've got to have help. In murder."

Pam made up her mind.

"All right," she said. "We'll come. But you must call the police. Ask for Bill Weigand—Lieutenant Weigand—and say I told you to. And we'll come. Where?"

The girl on the telephone gave the address.

"The police," Pam repeated. "Right away. Before anything else, remember."

"All right," the girl said. "Lieutenant Weigand."

The voice sounded not quite so shrill and breakable. "We'll come," Pam promised again, and hung up the telephone. She stood for a moment, looking at it. Then she turned quickly and hurried down the hall to Jerry's room. He was looking through his brief case for something. He looked up.

"Well," he said. "Welcome."

"Jerry," she said. "We've been called in. Just as if we were detectives. Mary Hunter's found a body. Come on."

"Wait," Jerry said. "I mean—wait. We've been—what?"

"She wants us to help," Pam said. "And she's calling Bill and we've got to hurry. Come on. Come *on!*"

Jerry looked at her and slowly he grinned.

"Look, dear," he said. "Before we rush into anything—or out anywhere—don't you think—"

"Jerry," she said. "I promised. Right away."

"Don't you think," Jerry repeated, "that you'd better put some clothes on? Particularly if the police are going to be there?"

Pam looked at herself and was honestly amazed at what she saw.

"Oh!" she said. *"Jerry!"*

• 2 •

TUESDAY, 6:10 P.M. TO 7:20 P.M.

The police photographers took their last shots and were reluctant, like all photographers, to admit that they had had enough. They stowed cameras and withdrew to stand by. The Assistant Medical Examiner was a thin, studious man in his forties and he knelt beside the body, took its temperature and examined it. Three slugs had gone into the chest, and any one of them would have been enough. There were no powder burns. The Assistant Medical Examiner said that whenever they were done with it, he was done with it—in its present place and position. For the record, he said, it was dead. Recently dead. Within an hour or so. That was as close as they need expect him to come, now or later, although he would look it over at the morgue.

The detective captain from the precinct said, "Thanks." He nodded to two detectives with weathered, out-of-doors faces, and they knelt by the body. They rolled dead fingers on an ink pad and on strips of paper, and made notations. They finished with ten fingers, and a man in a white coat from the morgue put a tag on the body. He and another man stood up and looked waitingly at the detective captain from the precinct. The captain knelt by the body and turned out the pockets. He gave the man from the morgue a scrawled receipt. The man from the morgue and his assistant put the body in a long basket and carried it out.

"They walk in and we carry 'em out," the man from the morgue observed to his assistant as they went down the narrow hall to the door. "Yeah," said the assistant, without emotion. He indicated he had heard it before, a touch of philosophy appropriate to the circumstances.

Bill Weigand, getting off the elevator, had to flatten himself against the wall to let the basket pass. They were hurrying it up, he decided, not pleased. When the basket passed he went into the apartment and raised eyebrows slightly at Sergeant Mullins, who raised shoulders slightly at the man from Homicide. His shoulders said that the precinct was in charge and where the hell had Lieutenant Weigand been? Weigand looked at the precinct captain and said, "Hiya, Jim," in a tone which expressed no interest whatever in Jim's health.

"Hi," Jim said. "You want it now?"

"Any time," Weigand told him. "Any time. Assuming somebody plugged him. You moved it right along, didn't you?"

"Well," the precinct captain said, "you wanted to look at it? Particularly? We made some mighty pretty pictures."

It would be all right with him, Bill Weigand thought, if nobody got killed in Capt. James Florini's precinct—with, possibly, the exception of Capt. James Florini. However—

"Can't leave them lying around all night," Captain Florini pointed out.

"Right," Weigand said. "I was tied up."

He hadn't been. It was hard to imagine any way he could have got there quicker, not being at precinct headquarters around the corner. But there was no sense in debating it. He turned away from Captain Florini, just not pointedly, to Sergeant Mullins.

"Well, Sergeant?" he said.

"Well," Sergeant Mullins said, "we just got here ourselves, Loot. Me and Stein and the other boys. The captain here had it pretty well taped out." He looked at the captain blandly. "Expeditious," he pointed out. "Like the man says."

"Right," Weigand agreed.

"Very high-class corpse," Mullins told him. "Only full of holes. Somebody did very nice shooting, Loot. From in front."

"Here," Captain Florini said. He pointed to objects laid out on a table. "Out of the pockets. You want to give me a receipt, Lieutenant?"

Weigand gave him a receipt. Captain Florini put it in his pocket.

"In your lap, Weigand," he said. "We'll send the stuff through. You can have it."

The tone was mildly pleased. Bill Weigand looked at him and waited.

"Merle," Captain Florini said. "George Merle. As the sergeant says, very high class. They picked it up in the press room and AP local's flashed it. You'll have company, Lieutenant. Also, he was a friend of the commissioner's. And of the mayor's. And probably of the governor's and for all I know of Mr. Big."

He looked at Weigand and smiled.

"So there it is," he said. "On a platter. Nothing in it for us precinct boys."

Weigand's face showed nothing. But his "Right" could be taken any way you chose. He crossed the little room to the table and looked down at the objects on it without touching them. Keys, a little pile of change, a notebook, a billfold which was comfortably swollen, a card case, a cigarette case, a silver lighter, two envelopes which had been slit open, a gold pocket watch, a case for glasses, a folding handkerchief, a fountain pen, two match folders, a folding checkbook in a case, a small pile of pieces of paper of anomalous purpose. He pulled a chair over and sat down.

"They haven't been printed," Florini told him.

"Right," Weigand said.

He handled them gingerly, touching only edges and protuberances. The billfold first. Its bulge was attributable to tens and twenties, which Weigand did not count. There was a secondary bulge of identification cards and papers. There was an operator's permit made out to George Merle of Elmcroft, Long Island; there was George Merle's owner's license for a Cadillac, 1942, convertible sedan. There was a sixty-trip commuter's ticket to Elmcroft, if Mr. Merle's gas ran out, but there was a folder of C gas coupons, so it probably wouldn't. There were a number of cards which testified to Mr. Merle's membership in a number of institutions. It looked as if the corpse had been that of Mr. George Merle. The card case held engraved cards in two compartments, social and business. Unquestionably, the corpse had been that of Mr. George Merle—of George Merle, President, Madison Avenue Bank and Trust Company. Everything beautifully in hand, beautifully in order. Except for the three holes in Mr. Merle.

It was enough to go on with. He turned from the desk, and Captain Florini and the precinct men had gone. Weigand looked at Mullins and smiled slightly.

"Phooey," Mullins said. "And double phooey."

"Right," Weigand said. "Coöperation, Mullins."

He looked at the girl for the first time, although he had seen her from the first. She was sitting in a corner of a little sofa and she made herself small. She looked at him and her eyes were wide and shocked.

"Now," Weigand said to her. "You found him? You're"—he looked at a slip of paper from his pocket—"Mrs. Richard Hunter? This is your apartment?"

The girl opened her mouth to speak and her voice caught. She swallowed and said, "Yes."

She was a pretty girl—slender, with blond hair cut boyishly but twisting slightly in a wave; her eyes were blue and she wore a dress of a paler blue. Just now she was pale; just now her eyes were wide and shocked. Her slender hands held tightly to one another and moved in a clenched embrace. Weigand noted but did not comment. A pretty, frightened girl. With a dead man in her apartment.

"You live here alone?" he said. It was hardly a question.

"Yes," the girl said. "Did you get my message?"

"That Pam North told you to call me—me, personally? Yes. You know Pam?"

"No," the girl said. "Not really. I met her and her husband at a party. I talked to her some. But they told me about her—about her experience with—this sort of thing. About her knowing the police."

"Right," Weigand said. "You live here alone, Mrs. Hunter. Your husband is—away?"

You could guess her husband was away. Husbands of girls her age were mostly away.

"He's—dead," she said. "Rick was killed in the Pacific. It was in the papers, about him. He—."

Bill Weigand said he remembered. He did remember. It had been memorable.

"I'm sorry," he said. "I didn't know, of course. So you do live here alone?"

Mary Hunter told him about that. As of yesterday—technically, if you preferred, as of Saturday. She had slept in the apartment the night before but only today was really moving in.

"They aren't my things," she said, looking around. "Nothing here is mine." She paused. "Nothing," she said. "I don't know about any of it."

"Right," Weigand said. "You walked in and he was lying here. You'd never seen him before?"

She hesitated. After the hesitation she did not need to say she had seen him before.

"A long time ago," she said, "I knew his son. Years ago, before I met Rick."

"And you knew Mr. Merle, too?" Weigand said. It was a statement.

The girl nodded.

"He was Josh's father," she said. "I went there weekends a few times. That was the only way I knew him."

Weigand looked at her, waiting.

"The *only* way," she said. "I know how it looks and—."

"It's just a coincidence?" Weigand said.

"It's got to be," the girl said. "I haven't seen him in—oh, for a long time. Except—."

She stopped and Weigand waited.

"Not for a long time," she said. "Two years, anyway. I think Rick and I ran into him once at a restaurant somewhere. That's all."

It was all for now, anyway, Weigand decided. He asked her to tell him about finding the body.

She had, she said, come home with some things and walked into the hall and there he was. You could see him from the hall. He had fallen in full view from the hall—on a straight line. And she had dropped the package.

"And screamed?" Weigand said.

"Yes," the girl said. "I must have. But I don't remember."

"And recognized him?" Weigand said.

The girl nodded, without speaking. She had a fine head, Weigand noticed.

"And then," Bill Weigand said, "you called Mrs. North. Why?"

"Because—I told you," the girl said. "I had met her and they said she—"

"No," Bill said. "I mean why did you call her? Instead of the police. How did you happen to think of calling her first? When you'd met her only casually, and knew only casually that she knew me. She's not a policewoman, you know. And her husband isn't a detective. They're just friends of mine."

"I don't know," the girl said. "I guess I thought they were detectives. Private detectives or something."

"He publishes books," Weigand said. "Didn't you gather that, at the party? When people were talking about them? And she—oh, works for the Navy League and things like that. Who told you they were detectives?"

"I don't know," Mary Hunter said. "Maybe I didn't think they were really detectives. I—I just thought of them."

Bill Weigand let it lie. He let it lie heavily.

"When did you recognize Mr. Merle?" he asked, after a moment. "When did you know it was somebody you knew? From the first?"

"No," the girl said. "Not from the first. Not until I went in and—and looked. Closely. Then I recognized him."

"And you didn't scream," Weigand said. "Or did you."

"I must have," she said. "I—I was frightened. And—I guess horrified."

Weigand looked at Mullins. Mullins shook his head.

"Not according to the guy on the elevator," Mullins said. "He'd just brought her up. He says he would have heard her and he says he didn't."

"Would he have heard you, Mrs. Hunter?" Weigand asked. "If you had screamed?"

The girl shook her head and said she didn't know.

"How can I tell?" she said. "What difference does it make?"

"Well," Bill Weigand said, "look at it this way. Here you are, a young woman coming home with things for dinner. You walk into your apartment and a man is lying dead on the floor. With blood around him. Why wouldn't you scream?"

"I don't know," the girl said.

"You wouldn't scream if he were still alive," Bill pointed out. He spoke softly. "Now would you, Mrs. Hunter? If he were—just standing there and you recognized him."

"And then shot him," the girl said. "Is that what you mean?" She paused. "And I suppose the elevator man would have heard a scream, but wouldn't have heard three shots?"

Weigand smiled. His smile was not friendly.

"Not if he had gone on down," he said. "If there had been—say two or three minutes intervening. As probably there would have been."

"Wherever he was, he would have heard shots," the girl insisted.

Weigand shook his head.

"The trouble with that is that he didn't," he told her. "I don't know why, but he didn't. He thinks he wouldn't if he were four floors down, or if he did would mistake the sound for a truck backfiring. In any case, he didn't. And shots were fired. Obviously."

The girl showed spirit.

"Not by me," she said.

"Right," Weigand said. "It's all a coincidence. You rent an apartment, a man you used to know picks it to walk into, somebody else shoots him. You're not connected at all."

"I don't care how it sounds," Mary Hunter said. But there was desperation in her voice. "Mrs. North will—"

"Mrs. North," Bill Weigand said, "is a very charming young woman who does work for the Navy League and is married to a man who publishes books. She is not—"

"Bill," Pam North said from the door. "How nice of you. Are we late?"

Bill looked at her and beyond her at Jerry. He said, "Hullo, you." He said no, they weren't late.

"It's nice to be charming," Pam said. "Where's the body?"

"In the morgue," Bill said. "Where would it be?"

"I don't know," Pam said. "As you were saying, I'm not a detective. Hello, Mrs. Hunter. This is Bill Weigand."

"We've met," the girl said. "He thinks I did it. He thinks because I called you I—." She stopped.

"Yes," Pam said. "I wondered about that too. It wasn't wise of you, if you didn't do it. Or, if you did." She paused and looked from Mary Hunter to Bill Weigand and back again. "Not that we're not interested," she said. "This is Jerry."

She gestured over her shoulder.

"Aren't we, darling," she said.

"Oh," Jerry North said. "Very, of course. How do you do, Mrs. Hunter?"

The Norths seemed to have animated her.

"Terribly," she said. "Your friend thinks I killed the old—Mr. Merle."

"The old what?" Pam said. She sounded interested.

The girl flushed.

"The old boy," she said. "Not what you think. Josh used to call him that and I—I did too. Because Josh did. Josh is his son, you know."

"Look," Jerry said, "we don't even know who got killed, or anything. Perhaps we'd better just go along and—."

Pam shook her head at him. She turned to Bill and said, "All right, Bill." Bill looked at Sergeant Mullins.

"O. K., Loot," Mullins said. "Sooner or later. Hullo, Mrs. North. Mr. North. They'll want to know."

Weigand looked at the Norths.

"Yes," he said. He said it with a certain inflection.

Mrs. North crossed the room and sat on the sofa with Mary Hunter. "All right," she said. Jerry still stood inside the door.

Weigand told them, economically, what he knew. He was impartial about Mary, telling what she had said. He told about the scream which was not screamed. When he had finished, Pam North's forehead was wrinkled. She looked at Mary Hunter and waited.

"I don't know," Mary said. "I seem to remember screaming, but maybe I merely screamed in—in my mind, sort of. If the old man was where he would have heard me, and says I didn't, then I didn't. Maybe I'm not the screaming type. I didn't scream when I—when I heard about Rick."

"Nobody knows, Bill," Pam North pointed out, looking at him. "Although if I came in and saw—what she saw—I'd scream. Wouldn't I, Jerry?"

"For the record," Jerry said, "you didn't. When it was in the bathtub. You just kind of made sounds—it was a kind of incredulous moan. But of course, it wasn't our bathtub."*

"Didn't I?" Pam said. "I thought—. You see how it could have been, Bill. And where's the gun?"

Bill Weigand said he didn't know. He added that there had been time enough to do something with a gun.

"Such," Pam said, "as what? What do you do with a gun? Mary hasn't got a gun. Or have you?"

"Yes," Mary said. "In my trunk. Under things. It was Rick's and when he left he—left it with me."

"Is it?" Pam asked, of Bill Weigand.

It was the first he had heard of it, Bill told her. They were in at the beginning.

"I could—" Mary began, but Bill shook his head. He nodded to Mullins and Mullins held out his hand. Mary Hunter found her keys and gave them to Mullins and pointed at a key and at the trunk. It was a steamer trunk and Mullins unpacked it methodically, thinking that women certainly needed a lot of underwear. He got to the bottom and looked at Bill and said, "No."

"Well," Weigand said, "there we are. No. Well, Mrs. Hunter?"

---

* The Norths found a body in a bathtub in *The Norths Meet Murder.* It was their introduction to murder, and to Lieut. William Weigand.

The slender girl with the short blond hair merely looked blank. She did not, so far as Bill Weigand could tell, look frightened.

"Then I don't know," she said. "I thought it was. I never used it." She paused. "For anything," she said. "Not since Rick—taught me to use it. I must have put it in something I stored."

"Anyway," Pam said, "she didn't have it today."

"Why?" said Jerry.

"Where?" said Pam. "I mean—where? In with the groceries? In a holster? Where?"

Jerry looked at the girl in the close-fitting blue dress. He saw what Pam meant. He looked at Bill Weigand. Bill shook his head.

"Obviously," he said, "if we decided she didn't find the body as she says, then we don't need to believe anything she says. It may have been—oh, in the icebox with the soda and she may have gone out ostensibly to mix a drink and come back with it. And she may—hell, she may have thrown it out the window."

He broke off and looked at Mary Hunter who merely looked back, with an expression which was half shrug.

"Drop that, for the moment," Bill said. "We can only guess until we look. The boys will look."

They could, he said, take up something else. She had rented the apartment on Sunday, day before yesterday. She had moved in— when? Yesterday afternoon? Very well, she had moved in yesterday afternoon, and everything was ordinary and routine. Right?

"Yes," the girl said.

"Who did you rent the apartment from?" Weigand asked. "An agent?"

The girl shook her head.

"A man I knew," she said. "A man I used to know in—in an office." She hesitated and they all noticed it.

"What office?" Bill Weigand said.

Mary Hunter wanted to know what difference it made.

"I don't know," Bill told her. "Apparently it makes a difference. To you." He stopped a moment and looked at her.

"Listen, Mrs. Hunter," he said. "I'm not trying to trap you. I'm not trying to do anything but find out the facts. If you didn't kill Merle, don't make me drag facts out of you. If you did—well, if you did, there's the telephone. Call a lawyer."

He waited as if he expected her to cross the room to the telephone. She did not move.

"All right," she said. "It was at the bank. Mr. Merle's bank. Right after Rick went away I—I had to find something to do. Everybody was working at something. It wasn't much of a job, because I couldn't do anything." She paused. "But I can now," she said. "I'm a secretary now. I went to school."

"Right," Weigand said. "Go on."

"Mr. Murdock worked there," she said. "He was sort of an assistant to Mr. Merle. Like a—like a secretary, but not a stenographic secretary. That was—oh, a year and a half ago. Right after Rick went. When I—heard about Rick I didn't go back. I didn't want to go anywhere."

She paused, as if waiting. Nobody said anything.

"I don't have to work," she said. "For the money, that is. Father left me some money."

There was another pause and she did not go on.

"Right," Weigand said, after they had waited. "Now about the apartment. You had kept in touch with this—Murdock, did you say? And you asked him if he knew anybody who had an apartment to rent?"

The girl shook her head. She said it hadn't been that way, exactly. She had run into Murdock quite by accident and he had asked what she was doing and she had said she had a new job, beginning Monday.

"That was last week," she said. "Yesterday was the Monday I meant. And he said, 'You don't want a new apartment to go with it, do you?' And I said I might, and did he know of one. He said he was just moving and wanted to sublet his and that I could have it Sunday if I wanted it. And I went and looked at it and it was all right, because of the way I wanted to live for a while. And so—this is it." She paused and half smiled.

"Only," she said, "it isn't the way I planned."

Under other circumstances, Pam thought, Mary Hunter would be gay. As she must have been gay with Rick, from the way her voice changed when she spoke of him. Not, Pam decided, that she wasn't getting over that, in a way.

Bill Weigand did not appear to notice Mary's last remark.

"So until day before yesterday, this apartment belonged to a man named Murdock," he said. "Any first name?"

"Oscar," Mary said. "Mr. Merle called him Ozzie, but his name was Oscar. On the roster. Oh!"

"Yes, Mrs. Hunter?" Bill Weigand said.

The girl's eyes seemed brighter, more animated. She leaned forward a little and spoke eagerly, in a very young voice.

"Couldn't Mr. Merle have come to see Mr. Murdock?" she said. "Couldn't that be it? Perhaps not knowing Mr. Murdock had moved? I mean—isn't that the real connection, somehow? Mr. Murdock did all sorts of things for Mr. Merle—confidential things."

Jerry North, half leaning by the door, nodded slowly. The girl saw his nod. Her eyes appreciated it. Jerry discovered that his eyes were appreciating her.

"It could be," Bill Weigand told her. "Obviously. We'll have to see Mr. Murdock. We'll have to see lots of people, Mrs. Hunter."

She was confident again, Weigand noticed, or at least not frightened. She had hold of herself. So there was to be no quick break, which would annoy Deputy Chief Inspector Artemus O'Malley, a man easy to annoy. And a man who would not approve of this—this social method of investigation.

"At the moment," Weigand said, "there are too many people right here. I'll want to have you tell me some more things later, Mrs. Hunter, but for the moment we'll let them go. Unless you can tell me Mr. Murdock's new address?"

She shook her head.

"Right," Weigand said. "We'll find him. Now, for the moment, I don't want you any longer. But I do want your apartment. For an hour or so. Would you mind—?"

"Look," the girl said. "I live here, Lieutenant."

But her voice was not combative. Weigand said he knew. Also, he said, he could take her downtown for more questions and look at the apartment—or have it looked at—while the questioning went on. On the other hand, more simply, she could go somewhere to dinner or something, and come back later, when perhaps she could have the apartment. Although probably she had better count on living in a hotel for a few days.

"For always," the girl said, and suddenly she was staring at the floor where the body had been and she began to tremble. For always, so far as this apartment was concerned.

It was coming home to her, now that the words pressing against her had ended; now that Bill Weigand's mind let hers up again. The others could see that; Weigand had seen it often enough before, and the Norths had seen it a few times. Pam North put a hand on the girl's arm.

"It's all right," she said. "It's going to be all right." She looked at the men, and both had seen her expression before. "It's going to be all right," she repeated, in a different tone and for a different purpose.

Jerry North and Bill looked at each other. Pam had, not for the first time, extended asylum to the frightened. Pam had become an advocate.

And now, Jerry thought—and suspected that Bill thought too—there would be that further complication; a psychological complication which would affect him a good deal, and Bill not a little. With a gesture, because a girl was trembling, Pam North had decided that the girl was innocent. And now they would be plagued by an uncertainty whether Pam was working on intuition, and hence could be wrong—as she had been several times in the past—or was working on something which was, in an obscure and glinting fashion, logic. In the latter case she might not be entirely right but she was unlikely to be entirely wrong. And in any case she was to be reckoned with.

"And probably," Jerry said aloud, "get herself into trouble again."

"Probably," Bill agreed, evidently with no difficulty at all in understanding what Jerry was talking about.

"Or," Pam said, "keep you two out of it. Which also happens."

Mary Hunter looked from one to another of them and she was puzzled. Pam smiled at her.

"They're talking about me," she said. "It's a way they have. Why don't we all go to dinner or something?"

"I couldn't," Mary said.

"Well," Pam said, "you've got to go somewhere, and it's time for dinner. Or almost. It's almost seven. And Jerry and I didn't find a body and while we're both very sorry, there it is. Isn't it, Jerry?"

As far as he was concerned, Jerry admitted, there it was. Although, he added to himself, you couldn't deny that they might be about to dine with a murderer. Which, also, had happened before.

Mary Hunter looked from one to the other again, and stood up. She stood up to an inch or two over five feet and even Pam was taller.

"All right," Mary said.

She looked at Weigand, who nodded.

"Right," he said. His eyes met those of Jerry and he nodded again, almost imperceptibly. "Where?"

"Oh," Pam said, "I think Charles, don't you, Jerry. Or somewhere."

"Make it Charles," Bill Weigand suggested. It was something more than a suggestion.

"Charles it is," Jerry agreed.

Charles it was. Gus made martinis from a bottle on a shelf behind him and they tasted like the old martinis of another year. Gus's dignified cordiality was encouraging, relaxing. Mary Hunter, sitting between the Norths, sipped her drink slowly and was still unfinished and shaking her head when Jerry ordered a second round. But she had quit trembling in the cab which brought them from Madison Avenue to lower Sixth and she was not trembling now.

She was not trembling until a telephone had rung, somewhere, mutedly, and Hugo had gone to answer it, and gone out into the restaurant, and after a minute or two come back with a tall, dark young man who limped slightly.

Mary looked up, turning toward Pam to answer something Pam had said, and she stiffened and her left hand, moving convulsively, brushed her cocktail glass. Jerry, beyond her, caught it as it tottered and his eyes followed hers. The tall young man did not see them, and he was nobody Jerry had ever seen.

Mary turned as the young man limped past, keeping him in view, but not speaking. Her eyes were large and—Jerry thought—frightened. The young man went into a telephone booth and still she looked at him. He had closed the door behind him before she spoke, and then her voice was so soft and tremulous that the Norths could hardly hear her.

"Josh," she said. "Oh, Josh."

The young man came out of the booth and his face was changed and his eyes were far away. It had not been good news.

Without a hat, without looking at anybody, the limping young man went out of the restaurant.

Mary then came back and the Norths were waiting. She looked at Pam, and her eyes were very wide and frightened, and she was trembling again.

"Josh," she said. "His—his son. Joshua Merle."

The girl was not, Pam knew—the girl's voice utterly revealed—talking about someone she knew only casually. As, it occurred to Pam, she had seemed to be when, earlier, she had mentioned that George Merle had a son named Joshua, whom a long time ago Mary Hunter—before she was Mary Hunter—had known and who had taught her to call his father "the old boy."

• 3 •

TUESDAY, 6:55 P.M. TO 8:05 P.M.

On the east side of Madison Avenue, between Seventy-third and Seventy-fourth, police cars seemed to be piled like jackstraws. That drew the crowd. The crowd stood and stared at the cars and waited. On the sidewalk in front of the old building, with a window bowing out in front, marked discreetly JAMES SELDEN, ANTIQUES, containing, as discreetly, a chair and a mirror, policemen in uniform told people to move on. People moved sluggishly and stopped again and stared at Mr. Selden's sign. They stared up at the windows of apartments above the shop.

"Nothing to see," the patrolmen said. "Nothing's going to happen, bud—lady. Move along, now. Keep moving now."

Across the street photographers had found vantage point in a shop window on the second floor. They took pictures of the house. Other photographers, immune to orders to move on but gaining little by immunity, smoked cigarettes on the stairs which led up to the building entrance, spanning an areaway with barred, low windows. They flicked the butts away and lighted fresh cigarettes and kept the gear of their trade close where they could nudge it with their feet.

The ones without camera cases and with cards in their hatbands were reporters. There were only a couple of them, standing by. This wasn't it; the precinct house was it, or headquarters of the Homicide Squad. Depending. One of the reporters was very young and wore very thick glasses and leaned against the stair railing and stared at nothing. He didn't want to be there; he didn't want to be working for AP local. He wanted to be in an airplane. The other reporter was in his sixties and red-faced and stocky. He wanted to be in a bar, and was going to arrange it. The *Daily News* thought of the damnedest things for him to do. You didn't see anybody from the *Times* hanging around, or from the *Trib*. What the hell—did the city editor think somebody was going to murder old Merle all over again for the exclusive benefit of the *Daily News?* Or that Weigand was suddenly going to walk out with the guy who did it in handcuffs? Anybody who'd been around town more than a week knew that nothing was going to break here. And that they weren't going to let him or anybody else in to poke around the apartment. Did the desk think he was a bloody sleuth?

Two patrolmen guarded the entrance, one at the door and one at the elevator. James Selden, a sparse gray man seemingly overlaid with a coating of dust, looked out of his door and, by peering diagonally through the glass, could see the patrolman at the outer door. It was just as well that Mrs. Belknap had decided not to come and examine the authentic table he had found for her. The policeman would have startled Mrs. Belknap, if anything could. Privately, Mr. Selden thought nothing could. But the whole business would have annoyed her, and probably she would have decided that JAMES SELDEN, ANTIQUES, was shady and mixed up in things. Mrs. Belknap would not like to trade with people who got mixed up in things.

Mr. Selden wished, mildly, that he had taken a more ordinary show room—a modern shop, with a front door which was privately his front door and not shared by apartment tenants, who, it now appeared, would fall into the habit of getting themselves murdered. There was, unquestionably, something old-world about the setup he had, with the bow window on the semi-second floor and the general air of almost British reticence. People like Mrs. Belknap were—he hoped—persuaded to think that bargains lurked unobtrusively in seclusion. Which showed what Mrs. Belknap knew.

Mr. Selden went to the other side of the door and looked diagonally in the opposite direction. There was a patrolman at the elevator, doing nothing. Mr. Selden sighed. He pulled a green shade down over the glass of the door. The shade had the word CLOSED printed on it. Mr. Selden withdrew to his apartment in the rear, furnished comfortably with non-antiques. He lighted a lamp which had been made three years before out of all new materials and moved the box of cigarettes nearer. He picked up a lending library copy of *Goodbye, Mr. Chippendale* and began to read it, chuckling occasionally. It wasn't going to be good for business, but it was quite a book.

In the yard behind the building, men in plain clothes—and with weathered faces—went over the ground inch by inch. They investigated the contents of ash cans and poked into dark corners, now and then surprising a rat. They seeped into the basement under the building and looked in darker corners with the aid of flashlights and found crated furniture and Mr. Selden's workshop. Some of the things in the workshop would have surprised them if they had been in the antique business, but they had interest only in things of the very recent past.

They did not find the gun they were looking for, which was as good as if they had found it, in one way. Detection lies as much in discovering what did not happen as in discovering what did. They were not annoyed by the fruitlessness of their search; they were entirely dispassionate. They were finding out what was in the court behind the house, under the windows of the apartment Mary Hunter had rented from Oscar Murdock, and what wasn't in the court. It was all the same either way.

Mullins and Detective Stein attended to the apartment itself, while Weigand went over the things which had been taken from the pockets of the recent Mr. Merle. Mullins and Stein went over things thoroughly, opening Mary Hunter's luggage with Mary Hunter's keys; picking up her lingerie from the drawers of the bureau and from her trunk, and putting it back. They went through the clothes hanging in the small closet; they examined the papers and the checkbook in her brief case. Mullins whistled when he looked at the checkbook and showed it to Stein, who said, "Yeah."

"Hey, Loot," Mullins said, "look at this."

Weigand looked at it, turning from the envelope he held in his hand. It was a very pretty cash balance; very pretty indeed.

"Yes, Sergeant," Weigand said. "That's very nice. She said she had some money, you know."

"O. K., Loot," Mullins said. "She could have said it again."

He laid the checkbook with some other things—letters, bills, memoranda without immediately apparent meaning—which would bear further examination.

Weigand read over again the brief letter he had taken from the envelope. The envelope bore that Monday's postmark and had been addressed to George Merle at the bank. The letter had been typed on a sheet of white bond paper.

"Mullins," Bill Weigand said, and held the letter out. Mullins crossed the room and bent over it, not touching what Bill Weigand touched so gingerly. He read it and said, "Hey!" It read:

Dear Mr. Merle: Everything is fixed up, finally. L. will show up there about five tomorrow and a check will be O.K. But no shaving of the amount, L. says. Sorry. But apparently it is the best we can do.

                                                                     O. M.

The signature, as well as the body of the note, was typed. Mullins read it again.

"Murdock?" he said.

"Well," Bill said, "it fits. Oscar Murdock for O. M. and here for 'there' as the place Merle was, apparently, to meet L. Whoever L. is."

"But—," Mullins said. Bill Weigand nodded.

"But Oscar doesn't live here any more," he agreed. "Or had he forgotten?"

"Or," Mullins said, "maybe he hadn't forgot. Maybe he wanted the Hunter girl to walk in on it. Or—or maybe the Hunter girl is L. A nickname or something."

"I knew a girl once that everybody called 'Lovely'," Detective Stein said, leaning around Mullins to read the letter.

"My God," Bill said.

"I don't know," Stein told him. "After a while you got used to it and it didn't sound funny any more. Come to think of it, I also knew a girl everybody called 'Sweetheart'."

"You don't live right," Mullins told him.

"Murdock knew Mrs. Hunter was working," Weigand said, more or less to himself. "She stood to get home some time after five. 'About five' doesn't fit it too badly. She'd have been earlier if she hadn't stopped to shop. And the nickname wouldn't have to be 'Lovely.' Maybe she has a middle name and people call her by it—some people. Old friends or what not."

"As a matter of fact," Stein said, with interest. "She has got a middle name. And it does begin with L. Louise. It's that way on some of her papers and things. 'Mary Louise Hunter.'"

"And," Mullins said, "she's got a nice bank account."

Bill Weigand looked at him and waited.

"I mean," Mullins said, "maybe that's the way she got it. Maybe people give her checks."

Weigand nodded slowly and started to put the letter back in its envelope. Then he took it out, laid it flat and drew a faint pencil mark circling the place his thumb had been. He flipped the letter over with the point of the pencil and made another faint mark on the opposite side.

"Except in those two places, I don't think I touched it," he said. He raised his voice. "Connors!"

Connors came in from the bathroom, where he had been spraying dust on the plumbing fixtures and blowing it off. Weigand gestured toward the paper. Connors blew dust on it and blew it off. He pointed to a whorling outline which appeared on the edge, near the pencil mark.

"Mine," Bill Weigand told him.

There were other marks. Connors studied them through a glass. He waved toward the chalked outline on the floor which marked the previous resting place of Mr. Merle.

"His," he said briefly.

He flicked the paper over and dusted again. The powder adhered in the swirls of a print on the edge and on two other prints.

"Mine again," Bill said. "Thumb."

"Obviously," Connors said, distantly. "And his again. Nobody else." He regarded Bill Weigand. "I guess you wrote it yourself, Loot," he said. "O.K. for me to get back to the bathroom? We're getting all kinds in there. Including toes. Somebody turns the bathtub off with his toes. Or her toes."

Weigand gestured him away. Using the pencil, and touching as little as possible, he refolded the letter and put it back in the envelope.

"The little man without any fingers," he said. "Or with gloves on them."

"That," Mullins said, "I'll buy."

"And so," Weigand said, "Oscar Murdock writes a note to his boss, inviting him to come and get killed, and initials it—and then uses gloves to keep his prints off. Ingenious."

"Well," Mullins said, "it could be at that, Loot."

Weigand agreed.

"When first we practice to deceive," he said. "We may practice twice. If we have that kind of a mind. So policemen will think that somebody else wrote the letter and tried to pin it on us. But why not merely tell Merle and not write at all? Why not telephone him?"

"I'll buy that, too," Mullins said. "Whoever wrote it. Why write it at all? Unless somebody wanted to pin it on Murdock."

"Or unless that's what Murdock wants us to think, being in it anyway," Weigand said. "We'll just have to ask."

The telephone rang. Mullins picked it up, listened, handed it to Bill Weigand. Weigand listened and said "Right." He listened and said, "We'll be along. We're about through here. Ask him to wait, will you?"

He put the telephone back.

"The old boy's son has turned up," he said. "At the precinct. He says the precinct telephoned him that his father was dead. We'll—."

He broke off and began again.

"No," he said. "Sergeant, you and Stein go along and keep him company. Extend sympathy and tell him we'll catch whoever did it. And you might find out where he was around five, just for routine's sake. I'll be along later."

He watched them go. He wandered about the living room; stood for a moment in the door of the bathroom and watched Connors and the photographer at work. He paused at one of the windows which opened over the courtyard and looked down at the men who still scratched for secrets in the court. One of them looked up and shook his head and Weigand nodded and left the window. He took his hat, called to Connors to lock up and bring the key with him when he was finished, and went into the hall. The elevator lumbered up with the old man at the control. The old man said nothing, and started the car down.

"So you didn't hear anybody scream," Weigand said. "Or any shots."

"No," the man said. "Unless I thought it was backfires. Nobody screamed."

"Right," Weigand said. "Did Murdock leave an address?"

"Not with me," the old man said. "Maybe with his nibs."

"Selden?" Weigand guessed. "The antique man?"

"Sure," the old man said. "Don't he own the joint?"

"Does he?" Weigand said.

"Sure. Who else?"

"I don't know," Weigand said, getting out.

The antique shop was closed for the night. But there was a bell signal beside the door and Weigand pushed it. Nothing happened. He pushed it again. James Selden ran up the shade and looked out at him.

"Closed," Selden said through the door. "Come back tomorrow."

"Police," Weigand shouted through the door. "I want to see you a minute."

"Damn," Selden said, loud enough to be heard through the glass. He had a good voice for a dusty man. He opened the door and stood in the doorway.

"How long are these cops going to blockade me?" he demanded. "Suppose somebody wants to buy something?"

"Tonight?" Weigand inquired, mildly. "They'll be gone by tomorrow."

"All right," James Selden said. "I don't know anything about it. I didn't hear anything or see anyone. I didn't shoot the girl."

"What girl?" Weigand said.

"The girl who got shot," the antique man told him with asperity. "In the fourth floor rear. In Murdock's old apartment."

"No girl got shot," Weigand told him. "A man. A man named Merle."

"Merle?" the antique man asked. "Not *George* Merle?"

"Why not?" Weigand said. "Did you know him?"

"Everybody knew him," James Selden said. "Or knew of him. As a matter of fact, I did know him, slightly. I sold him a mirror. Authentic, too."

"Some time," Weigand said, "you tell me about that. It might be interesting. Tomorrow, maybe. Now—give me Oscar Murdock's address, if you've got it. And I'll quit bothering you."

"Why not?" the antique man said. It was a great house for questions, Bill Weigand decided. "Did he kill him?"

Bill was patient.

"Not that I know of," he said. "I want to talk to him, that's all."

"The Main," the antique man said. "Him and the girl too, I wouldn't wonder."

"Right," Weigand said. "I didn't know about the girl."

"His wife, he says," James Selden told him. "I wouldn't know." He paused and peered at Weigand from under his layer of dust. "Merle was here several times about that mirror," he said. "A couple of months ago, maybe. And a month or so before that he was here about a chair."

"Did he buy it?" Weigand asked.

"No," James Selden told him. "He said it was too damned uncomfortable." He paused and reflected. "God knows it was," he added. "Good night."

He closed the door.

The Hotel Main was dignified and had an air of permanence. It was the proper distance over on the East Side and on a proper street. Bill Weigand parked the Buick with careful regard for parking signs and the hotel doorman told him it was a good evening. Weigand nodded.

The clerk behind the desk also thought the evening good. Weigand wanted to see Mr. Oscar Murdock.

"Room—" he began, and also began a reserved gesture toward the house telephone. "Oh, Mr. Murdock," he said. "This gentleman—."

He spoke to somebody behind Bill Weigand and Weigand turned around.

"—was just asking for you," the clerk said.

Murdock gave, first, the impression of good barbering. He was of medium height and just over medium roundness and he had innocent blue eyes in an innocent pink face. He looked at Weigand and did not know him and his manner intimated that that had been, until now, his loss. His voice was gentle and encouraging.

"Yes?" he said. "Mr.—?"

"Weigand," Weigand told him. "Lieutenant. Police lieutenant."

The effect was not startling. Oscar Murdock did not blanch nor tremble nor otherwise show alarm. But for a moment his eyes changed. They seemed to grow more shallow; tiny muscles moved around them. All you could say was that his expression changed; you could not say, definitely, what his expression changed to. But his calling had not, Weigand suspected, endeared him to Mr. Murdock.

Murdock's voice remained bland.

"The police?" he said, questioning it. "You want to see me?"

"About Merle's death," Weigand said. "His murder, you know."

The change of expression was more marked this time. The man looked shocked and something more than shocked. Perhaps the something more might be called disappointment. But perhaps Weigand was imagining things.

"Merle!" Murdock repeated. "Not *George* Merle?"

Everybody seemed to think it must be another Merle.

"George Merle," Weigand said. "The banker. Your employer, wasn't he?"

"My God, yes," Murdock said. "Did you say *murdered?*"

"Yes," Weigand said. "The banker—*the* Mr. Merle. Murdered. Somebody filled him full of lead. Or full enough."

"My God," Murdock said.

"In," Weigand told him, "your apartment. On Madison Avenue."

"My God," Murdock said. "I tried to—." He stopped suddenly. "When was it?"

A couple of hours ago, Weigand told him. More or less.

Murdock told him it wasn't possible. Two hours ago he saw Merle at the office. He was just as always. Murdock couldn't believe it.

"Two hours ago somebody was using him for a target," Weigand explained. "Accurately. What time did you see him?"

"A little before five," Murdock said. "I can't believe it."

Merle had been, Weigand explained, killed a little after five. Now it was a little after seven—now it was seven thirty. Murdock had seen him nearer three hours ago. Murdock shook his head, still showing that he couldn't believe it, and that it was a tremendous shock. His expressions and movements were plain enough now; they represented a loyal employee, and possibly a friend, who was bewildered and grieved by sudden death. His attitude was correct, which did not prove that the small gestures and muscular movements, the look in the eyes, the hand touching the forehead—that all these did not grow out of emotions sincerely felt. Mr. Murdock appeared a man who did things in order, which did not prove insincerity.

"This is a great shock to me, Lieutenant," Murdock said. "You can have no idea how great a shock. He was a great man—a great friend."

Weigand expressed his sympathy.

"It was considerate of you to tell me—to come here yourself, I mean," Murdock said. "I appreciate it. Old G. M." He looked at Weigand and shook his head. "I feel I should have been with him—have done something," he said. "I did so many things for him, you know. It was more than a job."

Murdock was more confiding than was to be expected. Suddenly he seemed to think of something. It was as if murder as a reciprocal activity, requiring a murderer as well as a victim, had just occurred to him.

"But who?" he said. "Who would want to kill G. M.? Do you know who, Lieutenant?"

"No," Weigand said. "We're trying to find out. That's what brought me here, Mr. Murdock. I thought you might be able to help."

Oscar Murdock shook his head doubtfully. He said he didn't see how. Not that he didn't want to help. Of course, if there was anything he could tell him that would help—. But probably they already knew all about Mr. Merle that would help. Everybody knew about Mr. Merle. Except for the personal things, of course. There he might help.

"He was a dignified, generous gentleman," Murdock said. "He was of the old school."

Murdock liked to say things the easy way, Weigand decided. What old school? There had been a good many—some of them, from their product, reform schools. Probably Murdock really meant that Mr. Merle had been a very rich man, head of a big bank, director of numerous corporations, generous in fund drives, titular head of charitable organizations with professionals doing the work. All very right and proper, of course; not necessarily a subject for pæans.

The detective's voice was grave, reflecting none of this.

"I'm sure that will be very—helpful, Mr. Murdock," he said. "We'll be very glad to hear about Mr. Merle from one who knew him as you did. However, there are one or two more specific points. If we could sit down somewhere?"

Murdock said of course, with the air of one who has been negligent in hospitality. He led the detective to a small lounge, offered him a cigarette, rang a little bell on a little table before Weigand could stop him. He seemed to guess that Weigand had been about to stop him.

"I don't know about you," he said, "but I need a drink. Won't you join me?"

Weigand was gravely tempted. Weigand resisted temptation. He waited, smoking, while a waiter came and took Murdock's order for scotch and plain water. Double scotch, not too much water. He let the waiter go and then he decided he had waited long enough.

"Mr. Merle went to your apartment at your invitation, Mr. Murdock," he said, in a voice without inflection. "He carried your invitation with him."

Murdock looked unbelieving. Then he slumped a little in his chair, and began shaking his head decisively.

"Wait a minute," Weigand said. "I saw the invitation. It was a note. I'll tell you what it said."

From memory Weigand told Oscar Murdock what the note said.

"Signed 'O. M.'" Weigand said. "On a typewriter. 'O. M.' for 'Oscar Murdock,' obviously."

He stopped to let it sink.

"All right, Mr. Murdock," he said. "Be helpful. You said you wanted to be."

Murdock continued to shake his head.

"No," he said. "I didn't send him any such note. I don't understand it. It was somebody else."

"Named—what?" Weigand wanted to know. "Oliver Murphy? Orville Mansfield? Did Mr. Merle know dozens of people with initials O. M.?"

"But," Murdock said, "that proves it, really. When I sent him memoranda and things I didn't sign O. M. I signed Oz—an O with a kind of a wriggle which meant 'Z.' Because he called me Ozzie. It was—a sort of a joke."

"Was it?" Weigand said. "A funny joke?"

"All right," Murdock said. "That's all I can say. I suppose you're going to arrest me?"

"Do you?" Weigand said. "Well, you may be right. But there's lots of time. You'll be around, won't you? You weren't thinking of going anywhere, were you?"

"I—" Murdock said. He looked at Weigand. "I guess not," he said.

"No," Weigand said. "I wouldn't. That would make it too easy. You and your wife—by the way, is your wife around?"

"My wife?" Murdock repeated. "Oh—you mean Laurel. No, she—"

"Isn't she your wife, Mr. Murdock?" Weigand said.

"Of course," Murdock said. He looked at Weigand. "Well," he said, "no. It was just—simpler. Real estate agents prefer it."

"She was just—?" Weigand said.

"Precisely," Murdock agreed. He looked at Weigand and smiled, man of the world to man of the world. "After all, Lieutenant," he said. "It does happen."

Weigand agreed it did, frequently. It would explain a thing or two, taken that way. It would explain why a man of Murdock's presumable affluence, trusted lieutenant to a man like George Merle, would be content with the comfortable but unquestionably small apartment over the antique shop.

"Did she know Merle?" Weigand wanted to know.

Merle had met Laurel, Murdock agreed.

"Her name's Laurel Burke," he said. "I'd like to keep her out of this."

That was natural, Weigand said. It did him credit. It was not likely to be possible. Particularly as the apartment was more hers than Murdock's.

"Did Merle think she was your wife?" Weigand wanted to know.

"I introduced her as my wife," Murdock said. "I don't know what he thought. I don't know that he thought about it."

Apparently, Weigand decided, the two men had known each other only during working hours. There was no meeting of families to match the advertised meeting of minds.

"By the way," Weigand said and stopped. The waiter returned with the drink. Murdock said he needed it. Murdock proved it.

"Did you happen to know Mr. Merle's family?" Weigand asked, casually.

"Oh yes," he said. "Josh and Ann. They're his children. His wife's dead, you know. And his sister—Mr. Merle's sister. She lives at the place out at Elmcroft. And Jamie. It's going to be pretty tough on Josh and Ann."

Weigand agreed that it was a very sad thing. He thought that Murdock knew more about Mr. Merle's domestic life than Merle had known of Murdock's. Which might very well be the way it would work out, considering their respective positions. If Merle were of an old enough school.

Murdock seemed ready to go on about the Merle family, but Weigand did not encourage him. They would have to be met—Joshua Merle was even now waiting to be met. Weigand summed it up.

"So you did not write Merle a letter telling him to come to the apartment. Right? You have no idea why he happened to go there. Right? You know nothing about his murder?"

"That's right," Murdock said.

Weigand said he hoped so.

"And he wasn't in the habit of dropping in at your apartment, I gather—at Miss Burke's apartment. Since he had only met Miss Burke casually. Right?"

"I don't think he was ever there," Murdock said. Weigand watched his eyes. Just for a second Murdock's eyes grew shallow again. "I didn't spread it around. I don't see how—"

"Right," Weigand said. "We know where we stand, at the moment. You'll understand that this is only the beginning as far as you're concerned, Mr. Murdock. You'll understand that there's still a lot to explain—a lot for you to explain." He stood up and looked down at Murdock. "I could arrest you now," he said. "I could make it stick, maybe. I'm not, simply because there is too much still to be cleared up. But stick around."

Murdock's barbered round face sagged. He nodded without speaking.

"And," Weigand said, "I want Miss Burke's address. I want to see her—and I don't want you seeing her until I do. Or communicating with her. If I find out you have—and I will find out—I'll have you picked up on suspicion. Is that clear?"

"All right," Murdock said. "That's clear."

Weigand wished it were quite that clear, really. He wished he knew how he was going to keep Murdock from getting in touch with Laurel Burke—how he was going to find out if Murdock did. There was just a chance that Murdock might credit him with clairvoyance and be afraid to risk it.

He noted down the girl's address.

"Is her name still Mrs. Murdock?" he inquired politely.

Murdock nodded.

"Right," Weigand said. "I'll be seeing you."

This promise did not enliven Murdock perceptibly. As Weigand walked away he heard the little bell on the table tinkle anxiously. Murdock needed sustenance. That was fine.

Weigand stopped at a telephone booth. He arranged to have Laurel Burke's apartment picketed from without; he arranged to have a man attend on Mr. Murdock at the earliest possible moment. If the two got together the men were to move in, break it up and bring both to Weigand's office. Otherwise, no action at the moment.

Then he telephoned Charles and chatted with Hugo, who answered. Hugo wanted to know when the Lieutenant—Hugo promoted him to captain, out of cordiality—was coming around. Hugo said the lobsters were good again and indicated that Gus was pining for the lieutenant's familiar face. Hugo summoned Jerry North.

The girl was still with them. Jerry would tell her that her apartment was not available, but that she could get such personal things as she wanted from it by application. He and Pam would take her to a hotel and remember what hotel.

"Any hotel except the Main," Weigand requested.

"O.K., Loot," Jerry North said broadly. "Wait a minute. Here's Pam."

"Bill," Pam said. "The old boy's son was here. Josh. A while ago. And somebody telephoned him and afterward he looked as if he had heard. And the girl knows him better than I thought."

"Does she?" Weigand asked. "How well did you think?"

"Oh," Pam said. "Just a long time ago, a little. But I think now it was a lot. And not such a long time ago. Anyway, in her mind. Because she looked like that."

It was quite a way to look, Bill told Pam. Mary Hunter must have an unusually expressive face. Pam told him all right, to wait and see. Bill promised that he would.

There were a good many coincidences around, Bill Weigand thought as he got into his car and headed for the precinct. A good many people seemed to know a good many people, with a nondescript apartment on Madison Avenue as a geographical center. It began to look complex.

Or, as Mullins would certainly say, screwy. Which Mullins would attribute to the presence of the Norths in it.

• 4 •

TUESDAY, 8:35 P.M. TO 9:25 P.M.

Bill Weigand was the better for hamburgers from Hamburg Heaven when he went into a dusty room in the precinct station house and was looked at by two young men. Seated, one was obviously taller than the other—a man in his middle twenties, darkly good-looking, darkly morose. The other was slighter and shorter; he had red hair and a quick face. The dark young man looked at Weigand as if he were measuring him, possibly for a coffin; the other's eyebrows went up and his face moved restlessly.

But it was the dark man who spoke.

"Your man," he said, "tells me they shot father."

The voice accused.

"Sergeant Mullins," Lieutenant Weigand said, with no expression. "Detective sergeant. What he told you is correct, Mr. Merle."

"What the hell kind of a town is this?" Joshua Merle demanded. He stood up. Although he tried to hide it, his face was working a little. "He wasn't somebody you shoot."

It was an odd statement, but it sounded less odd on the young voice.

"I'm sorry," Weigand said. "You have my sympathy, Mr. Merle. We'll do everything we can—."

"It's a hell of a time for that," the dark young man told him. But his voice was not so combative as his words.

"Steady, Josh," the red-headed one said. "Hold it, fella."

"Right," Weigand said. "Take it easy, Mr. Merle. It's tough—but take it easy as you can." He turned to the young man with red hair. "You're a friend of his, I gather?" he said. "You give him good advice."

"He's Weldon Jameson," Merle said. "He's a hell of a good friend of mine."

"Right," Weigand said, mildly.

"I ran into him," Merle said. "Asked him to come along with me. He felt the way I did about the old—about Dad."

"That's right," Jameson said, quickly. "He was a lot of guy, Josh's dad."

The two looked at Weigand. They could hardly have been less similar, but there was a likeness between them. It was more than their youth; the likeness was hard to decipher. It was, possibly, a kind of readiness; a kind of expectation that things would be tough.

Then Merle took a step forward and limped, favoring his right foot. And Jameson sat down in the wooden chair from which he had risen and his right leg did not bend properly at the knee.

Weigand's glance which accepted this was quick, but Jameson's noting of it was quicker.

"Crocks," he said. "A pair of surveyed sailors, Lieutenant."

"So what?" Merle said. "What's that got to do with it?"

"Nothing," Weigand told him. "Navy—both of you?"

"Naval aviation," Jameson said. "We got out." He looked at his leg. "The hard way," he told it.

"Skip it, Jamie," Merle said. "For God's sake. You think I—."

The other looked at young Merle. The command was as clear as if he had spoken.

"All right," Merle said. "Sorry, Jamie."

"You wanted," Weigand said, "to hear about your father."

He told Merle about his father, accepting Jameson as an auditor. Merle limped once across the room and back and sat down again as Weigand talked. When Weigand had finished, he said he didn't get it.

"Assuming somebody wanted to kill Dad," he said. "I don't know why, God knows, but somebody did. What took Dad to that dump?"

It wasn't particularly a dump, Weigand told him. It was merely a small apartment. Apparently what had taken George Merle there was a letter from a man named Murdock.

"Ozzie," Joshua Merle said. "What would Ozzie—I don't believe that, Lieutenant."

"Neither does Murdock," Weigand told him. "Or so he says. There was a letter which seemed to be signed by Murdock, inviting your father to come to the apartment. Alternatively, he may have come to see Mrs. Hunter."

"What Mrs. Hunter?" young Merle said. His tone was unexpectedly hot. "Mar—Rick Hunter's wife?"

"Mary Hunter," Weigand agreed, interested. "Apparently you knew her."

The young man stared at him. He seemed to be looking through him.

"Did you?" Weigand said.

"What?" Merle said. "Oh yes, I used to know her. Before she married. She married a guy in the Navy. He was killed a while ago."

He said the last without surprise, as if only the time were a matter of importance; as if the fact of the death were entirely routine. But perhaps this was because his tone was now unexpectedly cool, as if none of it—and particularly none of Mary Hunter—were of importance.

"You mean it was her apartment?" Weldon Jameson asked. His voice held interest; a good deal of interest. "I thought you said it was Murdock's."

Weigand shook his head.

"*Had* been Murdock's," he said. "He'd sublet it to Mrs. Hunter. Technically, anyway, it was hers when Mr. Merle was killed there. And she found the body." He paused. "She says," he added.

"And you say she didn't?" Merle asked. His voice was still uninterested. Weigand wondered if it was deliberately uninterested.

He didn't say anything, as yet, Weigand explained. He merely sought information. He hoped, for example, that Mr. Merle could give him some. Or Mr. Jameson.

"I believe you live with the Merles, Mr. Jameson?" he said, and then wondered why he believed that. Then he remembered that Murdock had mentioned a "Jamie" in connection with the Merle family.

Jameson smiled at the detective; the smile lighted his face. It was also somehow derisive.

"I've—been staying there," he said. "For a few months. Since . . . "

Nobody interrupted him. He merely stopped with that. He looked at young Merle as if waiting for him to interject. But Merle seemed to be thinking of something much further away.

"Well, Mr. Merle?" Weigand said, when the dark young man still did not answer.

Merle looked at the detective and brought his thoughts back.

"I don't know what you want, Lieutenant," he said. "What do you want?"

"Information," Weigand told him. "I want to find the man who murdered your father, Mr. Merle. Or the woman."

"All right," Merle said. "That's your job. But I don't know. Jamie here doesn't know. Why don't you find out? What did you want me here for?"

Weigand said he hadn't, particularly.

"Then what did your man here—what did whoever it was here—telephone me for?" Merle said. "How did he know where I was, for that matter? And why drag me around here? Unless—unless you want me to identify him?"

There was that, Weigand admitted, or would be. But tomorrow would have done; there wasn't much doubt. Mrs. Hunter had identified George Merle; so had papers in his pocket. As he explained this, Weigand himself grew puzzled. Who at the precinct had called this rather surly son of the murdered man? Weigand picked up a telephone to find out.

A few minutes later he put it down, and now he was more puzzled than before. Unless somebody at the precinct was lying, nobody had called young Merle. An effort had been made to reach somebody at the Merle house, and only a servant had been reached. A little later, however, Ann Merle, the daughter, had telephoned and had been told of the death of her father. The precinct had, properly enough, considered the family notified.

"Who called you?" Weigand asked, after he had spent a fruitless moment looking at the telephone. "Who did he say he was?"

"The police," Merle said. "Just 'this is the police.' Why? Wasn't it?"

"Apparently not," Weigand told him. "Where were you?"

"At a restaurant," Merle said. "A place named Charles. Downtown. If it wasn't the police, who was it? I don't get it."

"Neither do I," Weigand said. He thought it over. He looked at Merle again. "Neither do I," he repeated, in a different voice. Still looking at Merle, he picked up the telephone. His glance dropped to the dial long enough for a long finger to spin out a number he knew well enough. He talked for a moment, making no effort to lower his voice. He thanked Hugo at Charles and replaced the telephone.

"But," he said, "somebody did call you. I don't know what he said. But somebody called you. A man."

"He said what I told you," Merle said, and his voice was hot again.

"Right," Weigand said, without inflection.

He waited, but neither of the young men added anything. Physically different, they were alike again, looking at Weigand, waiting for him to go on. He went on. He said, but not as if it mattered to him, that the attitude was wrong—the attitude of young Merle. It was, he said, getting them nowhere. He was a policeman; he was trying to find out who killed Merle's father; he could use Merle's help. Granted a mystery in Mr. Merle's presence; granted something odd which needed looking into. The result was that Mr. Merle was there. They would find out why eventually.

"Somebody worked it," Merle said. "For some purpose."

"Obviously," Weigand told him. "Obviously, Mr. Merle." He started to explain something and decided not to. Under a case, until it was solved, there was always something moving—something in the dark, with purposes of its own; something that slipped away from under the hand; something with purposes as clear to it, and as mysterious to others, as the burrowings of a mole, as the twisting and turning of a mole's tunnel through the earth. If you knew the direction a mole was going and put your hand down in the path, the soil pressed up against your hand. Signifying mole at work. In an investigation, such a movement as surely signified murderer at work. But that was his problem, not Merle's—not Merle's if he was above ground, or Jameson's.

"For the time being," Weigand said, instead of any of this—"for the time being, we'll skip that, Mr. Merle. Have you any idea what your father did today before he was killed?"

It took Merle longer to tell it than it would have taken him to tell it simply. But there was little to it. George Merle had left his home on Long Island about nine o'clock that morning and had been driven to the Long Island Railroad Station. He had caught the 9:25 to New York, and that had put him at the Pennsylvania Station about 10:20—10:18, if the train was on time. Part of this was guesswork on his son's part; he knew about when his father left; the car had returned at about the interval to be expected if George Merle made the train. There had been nothing said about his missing the train. And, anyway, he never missed trains.

Presumably thereafter George Merle went to the bank; that was to be checked at the bank. There was no reason to think he had not; if he had not gone to the bank, presumably the bank would sooner or later have telephoned to inquire about his absence. He had had lunch with his son.

"Yes?" Weigand said.

At about one fifteen, at the Yale Club. The luncheon had lasted around an hour and a half.

"Right," Weigand said. "Was that customary? For you and your father to lunch together?"

There wasn't, Merle said, any custom about it. They lunched together occasionally, when he happened to be in town. He was not in town often—certainly not every day. But it was not unusual, either his being in town or his lunching with his father. And after lunch his father had, presumably, returned to his office.

"And you?" Weigand wanted to know.

The younger Merle had left the Long Island house in time to catch the 11:01 to New York. He had arrived, he supposed, at around 12. He had done various things—

"What things?" Weigand said.

Both young men looked at him with the appearance of surprised interest, and Merle looked as if he might challenge the question. But it seemed to Weigand as if something passed from Weldon Jameson to the taller, somewhat older man, and as if this something checked him.

"I walked across town," Merle said. He paused and looked at Weigand. "I don't walk fast any more," he said. "I looked in some windows. I stopped and bought a couple of ties."

"At?" Weigand said.

At Saks, Merle told him. He had still had time to kill—it was about a quarter to one. He walked over to Madison and down a little way and into a news-reel theater. He stayed there until it was time to meet his father at the club.

He had planned to go back to Long Island after lunch, but when it was time to catch the train he decided he was not interested in going back to Long Island. Instead he had stayed on at the club, having a drink or two, looking over newspapers. He had tried to call a girl in town and failed to get her.

"She'd moved," Merle said. "They said they didn't know where."

He had met a man he knew slightly at the club and had a drink or two with him, and suddenly grown bored with him. He had remembered an engagement—"a phoney engagement," Merle said—and had gone out into the summer afternoon still without purpose. He had wandered about the city for a while, looking in windows, killing time. Then he had telephoned Jameson at the Long Island house.

"Without getting me," Jameson said. "I'd taken the 2:13 in. Do you want to know what *I* did, Lieutenant?"

Weigand didn't, particularly, so far as he knew.

"Anyway," he said, "one thing at a time."

Merle hadn't, it appeared, done much of anything with most of his afternoon in town. He had tried to ring up another girl, and she was out of town. He had stopped in at another bar or two and had another drink or two, and then gone down to Charles. He had had several drinks at the bar there and then dinner and then whoever it was called him on the telephone, and told him his father had been murdered. He had started out and had met Jameson just coming in. They had come to the station house. They were still at the station house.

"And where," he inquired, "does it get you, Lieutenant? Do you think I killed Dad?"

"I don't know," Weigand said. His voice was mild. "I shouldn't think so. I hadn't thought so, particularly. Did you, Mr. Merle?"

Merle made a remark. It was a truculent remark. He added a single word—"Snafu." Weigand nodded slowly, agreeing it was all of that. It occurred to him that Joshua Merle was younger than he seemed—younger than the twenty-six or twenty-seven Weigand would have guessed—younger, anyway, in emotions. Jameson, Bill Weigand thought, was looking at his friend with concern.

"Take it easy, fella," Jameson said. He turned to Bill Weigand. "You can't accuse a guy of killing his own father, Lieutenant," he said.

Weigand thought of saying that it was not unheard of and decided not to say it. Instead, in the most matter of fact of tones, he said that he had made no such accusation, even by implication.

"Mr. Merle came here voluntarily," Bill explained. "And not at my invitation, whatever someone may have wanted him to think. I haven't, at the moment, any suspicion of anyone. And I haven't any more questions to ask either of you, at the moment."

Having said that, he waited.

"Dad—the body—" Merle said. "Do you want me to—?"

Weigand shook his head. At the moment the body would be—not available—for identification. Bill saw no reason for explaining why. He would want formal identification from a member of the family, but tomorrow would do. He would want to talk to other members of the family. For that, also, tomorrow would do. At the moment—.

"Come on, Jamie," Merle said. "Let's get out of here." He moved, limping, toward the door. Jameson followed him, his limp as pronounced, but different. At the door, Merle stopped suddenly, and turned.

"I didn't mean to—to get tough, or anything, Lieutenant," he said. "It was a jolt. O.K.?"

It was, Bill told him, perfectly O.K. He watched the two young men go out the door. He wondered what had happened to them—physically and more than physically. Eventually, no doubt, he would find out. You found out so much when you were investigating murders. Particularly so much that did you no good.

Weigand went out of the dusty room and pulled the door to after him. At the desk he checked again. Still there was no record that anyone had telephoned young Merle at Charles to tell him about the death of his father. That was another thing that would have to be found out about, eventually. He started out and the telephone rang behind him. The desk sergeant called him back. Deputy Chief Inspector Artemus O'Malley, in charge of the Homicide Squad, was on the wire. The sergeant looked at Bill Weigand with a certain expression and Bill, curbing himself, looked back with no expression at all. He picked up the telephone and Inspector O'Malley rumbled at him.

Where the hell, O'Malley wanted to know, did Weigand think he was. The question was evidently rhetorical, and O'Malley did not wait for an answer. What the hell did Weigand think he was doing?

"Working on the Merle killing," Bill told him, in a reasonable tone.

"Well," O'Malley said, "what about it?"

"I don't know," Bill said. "Not yet."

O'Malley's rumble gained in volume, but did not grow more articulate. It was distant thunder on the telephone. Bill waited, making soothing sounds. The rumble subsided somewhat; the voice became almost plaintive.

"Listen, Bill," O'Malley said. "For God's sake, listen. This guy Merle wasn't just anybody. He was—hell, he was *George* Merle. He ran a *bank*."

"I know, Inspector," Bill said. "It's one of those things."

It damned well was, O'Malley told him. And ever since the slip went out the boys had been driving him nuts. "On account of it's *George* Merle," he explained. "The *Times* and the *Herald Trib* particularly. Even if there is a war on, the *Times* says, it's still *George* Merle. You know that guy Hardy."

Weigand grinned into the telephone, but kept the grin out of his voice. He did know Hardy, and that Inspector O'Malley was not really a match for him. Hardy was a good man at his business, which was finding things out whether O'Malley wanted them found out or wanted them kept in, or didn't—as was often the case—know precisely what they were.

"Yes, Inspector," Weigand agreed. "I know Hardy. Did you tell him that we had a dragnet out?"

"Have we?" O'Malley said, evidently before he thought.

"Well," Bill said, "I don't know that we could call it a dragnet, exactly."

"All right," O'Malley said. "What the hell are you doing? What are we going to tell the newspaper guys?"

"We might just tell them that we're investigating," Weigand said. "That Mr. Merle was killed less than four hours ago. That at the moment we haven't any idea—not even the lousiest little idea—who knocked him off."

O'Malley told him for God's sake not to try to be funny. He pointed out that the tabloids had already gone in and that the *Times* and *Trib*— and the tabs too, for their later editions—had to have something. He wanted to know whether Bill didn't know a story when he saw one. He wanted to know whether Bill hadn't ever heard of *George* Merle.

"They're good enough guys," Bill said. "Just tell them the way things are, Inspector. Tell them we're—oh, tell them we are questioning several associates of the late bank president."

"Yeah," O'Malley said. "I did. They wanted to know what kind of associates. Banking? Or."

"Or?" Bill Weigand repeated, when O'Malley stopped.

"Just 'or'," O'Malley said. "You know what they meant. It was that guy from the *Mirror*."

"What did you say?" Weigand wanted to know.

"I said there were a lotta angles," O'Malley said. "I told them we were looking into all of them. Why don't you arrest the girl?"

Weigand wanted to know for what. O'Malley suggested murder.

"What the hell," he said. "She was there, wasn't she? He'd come to see her, hadn't he? What more do you want?"

"Evidence," Bill Weigand suggested.

O'Malley began to rumble again. Weigand spoke before he thought, to check the rumble short of thunder.

"I'm keeping an eye on her, Inspector," he said hurriedly—too hurriedly. "The Norths have—" He stopped. But had not stopped soon enough.

"Do you mean to stand there and tell me the Norths are in it?" O'Malley wanted to know. "Is that what you mean to do, Lieutenant?"

It hadn't been. But there was no point in insisting on discreet intentions. Weigand listened, dutifully, while the thunder rolled. After some time he was permitted to hang up, on the understanding that he had to solve the murder of *George* Merle within minutes—fifteen at the outside—get Mary Hunter away from Mr. and Mrs. North and Mr. and Mrs. North out of the case, and send Sergeant Mullins immediately downtown with a report of progress for the press. Weigand looked at the telephone for a moment after he replaced it and sighed. In some ways, he thought, Inspector O'Malley was getting to be altogether too much like the elder Clarence Day. Life with O'Malley was something, too.

He got Mullins out of the detectives' room and sent him south, into the jaws of the inspector. He went in search of Laurel Burke, known sometimes as Mrs. Oscar Murdock. It would be interesting if George Merle, when he made his last visit to anyone, had thought he was visiting Mr. and Mrs. Murdock. It would be, perhaps, even more interesting if he had thought he was visiting only Mrs. Murdock, whose first initial was "L" for Laurel.

· 5 ·

TUESDAY, 9:30 P.M. TO 10:20 P.M.

Mary Hunter had seemed to be moving in a dream after Joshua Merle left Charles. She had finished her drink in a dream and eaten—or moved her food in a semblance of eating—in a dream. After one or two efforts by Jerry North which brought almost imperceptible, but unquestionably negative, movements of the head from Pam—they had left her in the dream. And having dinner with a sad, if pretty dreamer, haunted by her discovery of murder—and very possibly, Pam thought, by something more—had not encouraged either appetite or conversation. So the Norths had appeared almost as dreamy as the girl; it was evidently only absent-mindedness which led Jerry to order fresh martinis after they were at their table. Presumably it was only abstraction which led him to drink his thirstily, and his prolonged gaze at Pam's half-full glass after he had finished was evidently only the gaze of a man who was thinking of something quite different. He seemed quite surprised when Pam pushed the half-full glass toward him, but the surprise passed quickly, with the martini.

The girl had merely acquiesced to their suggestion that a hotel on lower Fifth Avenue would be handy to where they were, and when she walked between them—the necessary block or two—she might have been a sleepwalker. Only after she had registered and turned to the

Norths from the desk did she make an effort to shake the mist from her mind.

Then she tried to make her voice casual, or seemed to try. She said they had both been wonderful.

"It was an amazing thing for you to do," she said. "You must have thought I was crazy—to call that way on people I didn't know. To drag you into—into my mess."

Jerry said it wasn't anything. The girl said oh, but it was. Pam looked at both of them. She spoke suddenly, with no abstraction at all in her voice.

"Do you know," she said, "you talk as if we'd filled in at bridge. Or paid your bill at a restaurant because you'd left your purse at home. Or told you that Commerce Street is two blocks down and one to the right." Pam paused. "Only it isn't, of course," she said. "It's—where is it, Jerry?"

"Well," Jerry said, "it's not really down at all. It's straight across, just about where Fourth Street and Twelfth Street cross."

"You," Pam said, "are thinking of Bank Street. Not that it isn't perfectly natural—Bank—Commerce. But I meant the Cherry Lane Street. That's Commerce. And it's downtown, with a theater on it. Or used to be."

Jerry North ran a hand abstractedly through his hair.

"Look, darling," he said. "Who gives a damn where Commerce Street is? Except the people who live on it."

"What?" Pam said. "I don't understand. What makes you dislike Commerce Street? Except that you don't know where it is. Which is your own fault, if anybody's."

"Listen," Jerry said. "*Listen,* Pam. I *like* Commerce Street. I also like Bank Street, except when it runs into the stables, which it probably doesn't any more." He looked at her anxiously. "What on earth," he wanted to know, "are we supposed to be talking about?"

That, Pam told him, was just it. That was precisely it. What were they talking about? That was the whole point, and what she was saying. They were talking, as far as he could tell, about something casual—something entirely trivial. Like the whereabouts of Bank Street.

"And really," she said, "it's murder. We weren't filling in for bridge. We were—we were attending a murder."

She looked at Mary Hunter.

"On," she said, "invitation. Your invitation, darling. So now you have to decide."

The slender girl looked back at Pam North. She stood motionless, and her face was almost motionless.

"Decide what, Mrs. North?" she said.

"We can't talk here," Pam said. "Not really. We'll sit down some place." She looked at Jerry, who nodded. "In the bar," she said. "Because it's convenient."

She started across the lobby toward the bar. The girl hesitated, and Jerry seemed to hesitate with her. But his hesitation was not uncertain; it suggested. Mary Hunter followed Mrs. North. She sat down with them, but with no air of permanence.

"What you have to decide," Pam said, as if nothing had intervened, "is whether we're to drop out. As of now. And if we are—why did you call us in? Because it wasn't what I'd expect—what anyone would expect. Unless you knew us better."

The girl seemed withdrawn. She said she was sorry.

"No," Pam said. "It isn't that easy. As if it were a—a case of mistaken identity. You called us in because you were frightened—terribly frightened. And you were frightened because of more than merely finding a body. You were—you were frightened for yourself. Because it all meant something about you."

Mary Hunter shook her head. Her voice was low and she seemed to have trouble keeping it steady.

"I didn't know what I was doing," she said. "I do, now. It was an imposition. And it was unnecessary."

"Why was it unnecessary?" Mrs. North said. "Because now you're out of it?"

The girl didn't say anything, in words. Her eyes said something. Pam looked quickly at Jerry and watched him shake his head slowly. She waited for him to speak. He spoke gently.

"I'm afraid, Mrs. Hunter, that it isn't going to be that way," he said. "Pam's right." He paused and looked at her. His voice was even more gentle when he went on, but his words were very slow and clear.

"You see, Mrs. Hunter, you're not out of it," he said. "I don't know how to explain—you shouldn't have brought us in, perhaps. We're not detectives and—I hardly know how to say this—we—we aren't casual about murder. People can't be. People can't pick it up, find out things—too many things—and drop it. And walk away. If you hadn't called Pam—if you hadn't brought us into it all—that would be different. We wouldn't have any responsibility."

"And now," the girl said, "now you feel you have?"

It was hardly a question. It hardly needed an answer.

"You see," Pam said, "you've told us too much. By calling us—by things you've said—by—by the way you looked."

"When I saw Josh," the girl said. There was a kind of resignation in her voice. "I tried not to."

"When you saw Josh," Pam said. She hesitated. "You see, my dear," she said, "I had to tell Bill about that. You see I had to."

"I don't know," the girl said. "Perhaps you did. It's all—it's all wrong. I don't know what I thought—why I called."

"You called because you were frightened," Pam said. "You sounded frightened." Pam looked at her a moment intently. "And now you aren't," she said. "Or you're frightened differently."

"I'm not frightened," the girl said. "It was a shock—it would be a shock, wouldn't it? To find Josh's father there, dead—to find anybody in your apartment, shot, when you—when you just came home in the evening by yourself." She paused. "And what was he doing there?" she said. "Why there?"

Pam looked at Jerry, who lifted his shoulders slightly and said, "Precisely." He said nothing further. Mary Hunter and Pam waited a moment, and he still said nothing further.

"Anyway," the girl said, "maybe I was frightened. Just at first. I knew him—I used to know him, anyway. It was my apartment. I found him. I was afraid—I was afraid the police wouldn't understand."

"Precisely," Jerry said. They both looked at him.

"There's only one other thing they would want," he added. "A motive. Did you have a motive, Mrs. Hunter?"

The girl spoke quickly and said, "No—no, of course not." She said it so very quickly that Pam looked at her oddly, and then looked at Jerry. He, also, was looking at Mary Hunter, and he seemed to be waiting. The girl looked at Pam North and then at Jerry North and said the obvious.

"What motive could I have?" said she.

There was another little pause. There seemed, Pam thought, to be more pauses in the conversation than conversation. It was a pause—an uneasy pause—marred a little by words.

"Precisely," Jerry said. He seemed, Pam thought, to have taken a fancy to the word. She was sorry; it was not a word she much cared for. But she was not surprised to see that Jerry was looking at her with an evident inquiry in his glance, or that he was moving as if to rise. She picked up her bag.

"And since you haven't," Jerry said, "you naturally aren't frightened. Since you aren't frightened, you don't want us to—you don't want us as seconds, or whatever you had in mind. We're bound, as I said, to tell Bill Weigand what you've told us—and suggested to us. We don't have to go on with it."

He pushed the table a little aside and stood up.

"And," he said, "you probably want rest and quiet. And won't mind if we get along. All right?"

"I—" the girl said.

Pam stood up too. They waited a moment looking down at her. She looked up at them.

"I didn't mean—" said she, and broke off again.

"There wasn't anything to mean," Jerry told her. "You—you called a doctor. An amateur doctor, as it happens. You got well before the doctor came."

Pam laid a hand on his arm. He looked at it a moment and then looked back at the girl. And for a fraction of a second longer he waited.

"Are you well, Mrs. Hunter?" Pam said, beside him.

The slender girl looked up at them for a moment longer, and then she—very slowly—shook her head. And her eyes had tears in them—painful tears.

"I didn't kill him," she said. "I swear I didn't kill him."

"But," Jerry said, "you had a motive. Or something the police would call a motive, if they wanted to." He did not put the words as a question.

The girl nodded.

"Josh," she said. "Josh and I—"

But Pam was shaking her head.

"If you're going to tell us any more, you'll end by telling us everything more," she said. "And not here—perhaps not anywhere. What we know, Bill knows. At least—"

"Unless Pam decides it would confuse him," Jerry filled in, and he smiled faintly. "Which has happened." He sobered. "But if Pam means that we're not on anybody's side, as she does, she's right," he said. "If she means we're not protecting anybody."

"Except," Pam said, "if they didn't do it. And then, of course, we would be. Unless we were wrong, of course."

The girl looked at both of them, and shook her head again. She said she didn't need protection.

"For myself," she said. And then as if this might be misleading, she added more hastily. "Or for anybody," she said. "And there isn't much to tell. But—I'd like to tell you what there is. And you can tell me—well, if I ought to be afraid. And if I ought to tell your Bill—Lieutenant Weigand—about Josh and me and Josh's father."

"Still," Pam said, "not here. We'd better go up to your room, if you want to tell us anything."

"Without prejudice," Jerry said.

The girl smiled up at him.

"Without prejudice," she said.

The girl's room had one chair that was supposed to be comfortable, and one about which no one had supposed anything, except that it was a chair to put by a table and to be sat on by a guest who wanted—for whatever obscure reasons of his own—to sit by a table. There was a bed, with a reading lamp on the headboard, artfully placed so that a bed-reader's head would inevitably shadow his book; there was a telephone and there was a window from which one could look down on Fifth Avenue. Mary Hunter sat in the straight chair and Pam North in the other. Pam tried to sit on her foot and be comfortable, but there was no room in the chair. She tried it twice and gave it up. Jerry sat on the window-sill. He looked down at the street and it was a long way down, so he looked instead at Mary Hunter. She had very wide-spaced eyes; her cheekbones made her face a soft triangle. She would, Jerry thought, photograph beautifully.

She talked with many little pauses between her sentences and she talked more slowly as she went on, but also with less hesitancy. She remembered as she talked.

It had been—what there was of it to be—in the summer before the war. "The strange summer," she said, and Pam nodded. She remembered it as a strange summer—a restless summer, in which all that one did seemed tentative and merely a part of waiting; a summer in which nothing could be started that would outlast the summer; a time in which no one could keep his mind on anything that was, because it was so clear what was to be. And yet it had not been clear what was coming—not clear to the mind. There was a kind of disbelief in everything and nothing was quite real, even the approaching—the almost certainly approaching—reality of the future which was to change everything. (And which had, actually, changed only some things, and those only for some people.) But perhaps this was only, Pam thought, the way one remembered the summer; perhaps, for the most part, it had really been like any summer, no more desperate—except that now, knowing more clearly that it was the last summer of its kind, one felt it should have been desperate, and so remembered that it was.

And it could not have been so very different for a girl of nineteen—blond and pretty and living pleasantly on Long Island. Living only pleasantly, not extravagantly. "It was just a little house, really," Mary said. "Not like the Merles'. Dad didn't have money like that—he didn't have as much money as he used to have." But there had been the big car—the reasonably big car—and the station wagon. It had, Jerry North gathered, been more than suburban.

"Two or three years before that," the girl said, "Dad was—I think he was—making quite a lot of money. When I was about sixteen. Everything felt like he was making a lot of money. I guess I just took it for granted. Then, just before I was nineteen—that was in February—he told mother they'd have to pull in their horns. But when she looked worried and said, 'You mean really, Frank?' he smiled and shook his head and said, 'Not really. Just a little.'"

They waited, because she paused then.

"This has something to do with the rest of it," she said. "It's not—not just reminiscence."

They accepted her statement without words. She went on.

It had been that spring—the spring she was nineteen—that she had really met Joshua Merle. She accented the word "really" and explained. It was not, really—she smiled slightly at her repetition of the word—not really the first time she had met him. She must have met him a dozen times when they were both growing up, he a few years ahead of her in the process. The families had known each other—casually. "Or I thought casually," she said. "Now I don't know. Because Dad and Mr. Merle had some sort of business contact."

She shook her head and said she was sorry.

"That's all I know," she said. "I didn't think much about things like that. I didn't know anything about it at the time. The Merles were just people who—oh, who went to the same church Mother and Dad did and who had a lot of money and a big place, and who sent the best flowers when the church was decorated. That didn't mean much one way or the other, to me, because the church didn't. I guess it didn't to Dad, either, but it did to Mother."

Pam started to say something, but Jerry shook his head at her. The girl did not notice.

She had met Joshua Merle at a dance at the country club on a Saturday night. As she remembered it—as she remembered something—her face changed and her eyes changed. They had met in a big way. The words were hers. "We met in a big way," she said. "We didn't know where we had been all our lives—all one another's life—how ought I to say it, Mrs. North?"

"It doesn't matter," Mrs. North said. "The way you said it was perfectly clear." Pam looked at Jerry. "Perfectly clear," she repeated.

"At least as clear as—" Jerry said, and stopped. Pam slightly made a face at him.

"Josh—it's because of his grandfather," the girl explained. "The name is. Josh had been down from Princeton for the weekend. During the rest of the spring he was down for other weekends, and after he was graduated he was home.

"And we met a lot," she said. "An awful lot—we went riding and played tennis and danced and went swimming and—oh, all the things you do in summer." She paused. "Including falling in love," she said. "Which is something you do mostly in summer, I guess. Josh was—he was sweet."

She paused for a longer moment; it seemed that she was not going on.

"And something happened?" Mrs. North said, finally.

The girl looked at her.

"I—" she said. She stopped. "We were going to get married," she said. "We decided to get married. Before the war started. Because everybody knew it was going to start. But—." She swallowed and shook her head, so that the short blond hair was ruffled. When she continued it was with an effort to make her voice impersonal; it was with what seemed to be an effort to wipe out of her mind the knowledge that she was telling the story to anyone. She spoke as if speaking to herself.

"It was like—oh, like a melodrama," she said. "Some kind of a bad play. Josh took me to their place one afternoon and we were going to have a swim and a drink and then go on to dinner with some other people. And Mr. Merle sent word out to me by one of the servants that he would like me to come to his study. And I went. I was wearing a white play suit. I didn't feel grown up at all."

George Merle had been very formidable at a desk—a heavy desk with a sheet of plate glass over the top. He had sat behind the desk and he had said, "Sit down, Miss Thorgson." She had sat down and he had sat for a long minute looking at her and not saying anything. "And knowing what he was doing to me," the girl said. Then he had begun to talk.

He said that he was afraid she and Joshua were getting unfortunate notions about each other, and that he did not want her to make any mistake. He said this coldly and evenly, and without any particular inflection. He had sat behind the heavy desk and looked at the slight blond girl in a white play suit which made her—there, with him looking at her—feel helplessly like a child, and he had spoken evenly and without any friendliness in his voice.

"You think," he had said, "that Joshua has a great deal of money, or will have. No doubt your father thinks so too."

"My father?" the girl had said. "I don't know what you mean, Mr. Merle."

Merle had said that she knew well enough. That her father knew well enough. But he had no objection to putting it into words.

"You think that Joshua is worth marrying," he said. "No doubt your father thinks that is a good way to get it back. You can tell him for me it won't work."

The girl said that she hadn't understood. "I told him I didn't understand what he meant," she said.

"What I mean is," he said, "that you are planning to marry Joshua for his money—my money. Your father put you up to it, I imagine. But it isn't going to work. Because if he marries you he won't have any money. Now or in the future. He won't have his allowance. He won't get any money when I die." He had paused, then, thinking it over. "At least," he said, "he won't if I can help it. The way the courts are now, no sane man can say what they'll rule. But it would take him years—and for years he wouldn't have any money. You can tell your father that, Miss Thorgson."

The girl still hadn't understood.

"Even now," she said, "I don't know what he meant. But I think he hated Dad. It must have been something—something to do with business—that they were in together. I think it had something to do with Dad not having as much money as he used to have—suddenly not having as much money. But I don't know. I never asked Dad—I never told him anything about it. I couldn't. And then he died, that fall."

Then, before the implacable man behind the heavy desk, she had merely stood up, feeling white. "I must have been white," she said. "I felt so—so gone. And I said a very strange thing."

She paused, not hesitantly, but as if she were remembering anew.

"I said, 'You're horrible. You ought to die,'" the girl said. "I said 'You ought to die.' And this afternoon I came home and—and he was dead."

Her voice was distant; it had the distance of an echo.

· 6 ·

TUESDAY, 9:40 P.M. TO 10:15 P.M.

The surgeon worked under a bright light beating down on what had been Mr. George Merle. His instruments glittered a little under the light; he reached in with forceps and drew out what he had been looking for. He held it up under the light and examined it and dropped it into a basin, sloshing it. He picked it out with the forceps and looked at it again and nodded approvingly.

One slug which had terminated Mr. Merle had been much harder than Mr. Merle and was much less damaged. It would come in handy, Dr. Mayhew, Assistant Medical Examiner, decided. The ballistics men would not be provoked, as they sometimes were, by getting a battered slug from a battered cadaver. This one would please them; the marks of the rifling—yes, and the imprint of the firing pin—would show up nicely under their microscopes. All they needed now was another slug to go with it, which was no business of Dr. Mayhew.

It was almost ten o'clock at night, and the surroundings were unbeautiful. Dr. Mayhew sliced deftly at a pectoral muscle and whistled "Oh, What a Beautiful Morning." He sliced on. He dictated to an assistant, perched on a revolving stool, using a laboratory table for his notebook.

"Well nourished," Dr. Mayhew reported. "Did very well by himself, this one did. Had a couple of drinks before he got it. Had a couple of drinks every now and then, possibly." He whistled "I've got a beautiful feeling—"

"Late fifties," he announced, breaking off. "Could have done with more exercise, probably. Nothing the matter with his heart." He paused and looked at his work. "Except for the bullet in it," he added. "Cause of death—hmmm. Destruction of the left ventricle; gunshot wound. Second gunshot wound in right breast. Punctured lung. Third gunshot wound three inches below second. Deflected by rib—and seems to have lodged in the spine. Probably pretty badly mashed up— the slug. The spine too, as a matter of fact. Thirty-eight calibre—the slug, not the spine . . . " He whistled several bars of "The Surrey with the Fringe on Top." His assistant listened morosely.

"Hell," he said. "It don't go like that. It goes like this." He demonstrated.

"Usual appendicitis scar," Dr. Mayhew said, with increased firmness. "Weight 160. Height five feet, ten. The man, not the scar. Very good manicure, by the way. And he didn't use his hands much."

"Hell, no," the assistant said, jotting. "He was a banker."

"Was he?" Dr. Mayhew said, not much interested. He had another shot at "The Surrey with the Fringe on Top." "That way?" he asked.

"George Merle," the assistant said. "Banker *and* philanthropist. Fund chairman. Committee chairman. Board of Directors chairman. *President* of a bank. Come back to you, Doc?"

"I," said Dr. Mayhew, "am an assistant medical examiner. I don't get around—not with the live ones." He stood up and looked at his work, which had been thorough.

He dropped his tools in a basin.

"All right," he said, "you can tell the boys he's ready to go."

"Every available detective is working on the case," Acting Chief Inspector Artemus O'Malley said firmly. "Every available detective."

Inspector O'Malley sat firmly behind his desk and looked at the reporters with honest eyes. The reporters looked back at him with skepticism.

"Listen, Inspector," the man from the *News* said. "This isn't just some stiff who got himself conked. This is George Merle. You know who he is?"

"Certainly," said the inspector. "We are fully aware—"

"What we want to know," the man from the *Herald Tribune* said with great patience, "is where you're getting. Have you got any line on it?"

"Oh, yes," the inspector said. "We're making definite progress. We expect—"

"Look," the *Mirror* man said, "we write it that way, Inspector. You just tell us—we'll write it. Are you getting anywhere? Did he go to see the girl? Were they that way? Love nest?"

"You're damned r—" the inspector said, and remembered suddenly. "We are investigating all angles," he said, with enhanced firmness. He looked slightly harassed. He changed slightly.

"Listen, boys," he said, and he was a boy among boys. "There ain't—there isn't a thing I can tell you. Not for the record. You know that."

"What we want to know," the *Times* man pointed out, "is—do you *know* anything." He waited, as if for the inspector to understand. "You see," he said, "Mr. Merle was a very important man, Inspector. The public is interested in him because he was a very important man. They want to know what the police are doing about his murder."

Inspector O'Malley looked at them all, and his gaze grew slightly baleful. He looked hard at Sergeant Mullins, present as an emissary from Lieutenant Weigand, and Mullins, who seldom shrank, shrank perceptibly. Mullins was glad at the moment that he was not Lieutenant Weigand; he would have been reasonably contented not to be Sergeant Mullins. He felt like a buffer state.

"Our best men are working on the case," Inspector O'Malley said, mollified by the shrinkage of Mullins. "Look, boys—I'm working on it myself."

It had the form of an impressive announcement. But it did not have the effect of an impressive announcement. The *Times* looked at the *Tribune*. The *Tribune* raised eyebrows.

"How about Weigand?" the *Tribune* inquired.

"Weigand—the sergeant here—everybody," O'Malley told him. "Under my direction—my *personal* direction."

The *News* said, "Oh." The *News* used a falling inflection.

"Look, Inspector," the *Mirror* said. "How's about seeing Weigand?"

The inspector was about to answer, when the door opened. A uniformed patrolman said, "Here's a guy from *PM,* Inspector." Everybody looked at the guy from *PM,* who was rather small but very certain. He looked only at the inspector.

"Inspector," he said, "we hear that you've got two Negroes locked up in a precinct house charged with killing Merle. We hear you're beating the hell out of them. How about it?"

"We—" said Inspector O'Malley. "You—"

"You don't know," the guy from *PM* told him. "That isn't good enough for *PM,* Inspector. What are you doing to find out?"

"There isn't a—" the inspector said. "We haven't got—"

"'No comment'," the guy from *PM* said, with great sarcasm. "The good old 'No comment.' You can't get away with that, Inspector. Not with *PM* you can't. Frankly, my story won't let you get away with the 'No comment' gag, Inspector. Frankly."

The inspector stood up behind his desk.

"You," he said, "get the hell out of here!"

He said it with vigor. Mullins jumped slightly. The guy from *PM* backed away from him.

"Don't try it," he said. "Don't try it!" He spoke hurriedly. "Not with *PM.* I'll—"

He kept an eye on Mullins and edged toward the door. He reached it and put a hand on the knob.

"So," he said. "That's the police answer. You ask a civil question— as a citizen, as a reporter—and what happens?" He pulled the door toward him. "You get thrown out!" he said. He spoke bitterly. "You—"

Mullins had not advanced. But he twitched slightly.

"—get thrown out," the guy from *PM* repeated, even more hurriedly. "All right. Wait until you read—" Mullins twitched again. "*PM!*" the guy from *PM* said, loudly and defiantly, and leaped through the door.

O'Malley remained standing. He looked at the others.

"All of you," he said. "The hell out!"

They went, without hurrying. At the door the last of them, the man from the *Times,* turned back and shook his head sadly. He didn't say anything. After they had gone, O'Malley glared for a moment at the closed door. Then he moved his glare to Mullins.

Laurel Burke, known sometimes as Mrs. Oscar Murdock, would be all right to visit, Bill Weigand thought, looking at her. A good place to visit, but, like New York. Very much like New York, he decided—difficult to imagine in another environment. She was blond, perhaps by intention; she had a broad low forehead and widely set dark blue eyes; her chin was firm and rounded. Possibly, if you thought much about it, you might decide that her face was heavier than faces needed to be. But no man was apt to spend that much time in analysis, at any rate of her face.

Bill thought, almost hurriedly, of Dorian, who was known always as Mrs. Weigand and had eyes with greenish lights and fully as good a figure. Dorian did not have hostess pajamas of quite this cut—quite this daring—and would hardly have worn them if she had. It was a matter of taste, but there was a little of the carnivorous in all men. Probably there had been, for example, in George Merle. Which might account for—

Her voice was carefully low; intentionally low. She might, Bill thought, practice from time to time on it, keeping the pitch down. There was hardly a suggestion, and that not in tone but in inflection, that once it might have been a voice for use in subway trains.

"Well, Lieutenant," she said. "You'll know me next time?"

He was not disconcerted. He agreed gravely that he would. He returned attack with attack.

"Mr. Merle knew a good thing," he said. "You."

She widened her eyes in vast surprise and bewilderment. She narrowed them in realization.

"What the hell do you mean by that?" she said.

She still stood in the door she had opened when Bill Weigand rang the bell. Weigand waited but she showed no inclination to move.

"Do you want to talk about it here?" he said.

She looked at him, considering. Her eyes were suspicious.

"Let's see your badge," she said. "If you've got a badge."

Weigand showed her his shield. She looked at it and seemed convinced.

"All right," she said. "Come on in."

She swayed slightly and becomingly as she walked. It took all kinds of women to make a sex and she was one kind. Dorian would never allow herself to sway in just that fashion. It was a matter of taste, and a variety of tastes are possible to man. Laurel Burke's pajamas fitted tightly over the hips and flared below them. She wore black house shoes on bare feet and the shoes were cut to disclose enameled toenails. The pajamas fitted affectionately above the waist. She went to a sofa and sat without looking at Weigand. She stretched back in it, and the pajamas, cut low in front, tightened over her breasts. She looked up at Weigand.

"Very pretty," Weigand said, conversationally. "Very pretty indeed. As I said, Mr. Merle knew a good thing." He paused, looking down at her. "And don't ask me what Mr. Merle," he suggested.

She seemed unperturbed.

"I know a Mr. Merle," she said. "Slightly. Otherwise, I don't know what you're talking about. Except that you're talking like a cop."

Weigand pulled a chair up and sat on it. He waited while she finished.

"In case you don't know," he said, "George Merle was killed this afternoon. In your apartment."

Her eyes widened, she gave a small gasp, she leaned forward toward Weigand. She said, "No."

"Yes," Weigand said. "Somebody shot him."

He waited. She looked as if the news were a surprise, as if it were shocking. She looked as if she could, for the moment, think only of the central fact of George Merle's death.

"Oscar—it will be a terrible blow to Oscar," she said, as if to herself. She seemed to remember Weigand. "My husband," she said. "He was devoted to Mr. Merle. He'll—he'll be terribly upset."

Weigand made a sound which might mean anything and waited. She seemed to be recovering from her first surprise.

"Wait a minute," she said. "You said something else. Something about—" She paused, apparently trying to remember.

"I said he was shot in your apartment," Bill told her, patiently.

"Yes," she said. "That's what you said. I don't know what you mean. I've been here all afternoon—it's—"

"The apartment on Madison," Weigand said. "The one over the antique shop. Your former apartment, if you like that better. The one you had with Mr. Murdock. Your—husband."

She looked at him; her eyes measured him.

"Well," she said. "Well? I thought you were a homicide dick."

"I am," Weigand told her.

"You sound like the morals squad," she said. "Or something. Who says Ozzie isn't my husband?"

"Ozzie," Weigand told her.

She twisted her lips down; then she twisted them up, making it a smile—a derisive smile.

"Trust a man," she said. "Trust them not to be worth trusting. Ozzie's a heel."

Weigand had no comment.

"All right," she said. "The apartment I used to live in. As Mrs. Murdock—without being Mrs. Murdock. And Merle was killed there. So I suppose I killed him."

People jumped to conclusions, Weigand thought. His voice was tired.

"I haven't supposed you killed him, Mrs. Murdock," he said. "Did you?"

"Make it Burke," she said. "Miss Burke. No. Why should I?"

"Laurel Burke," Weigand said, not as an answer. "Laurel—beginning with L."

"The man can spell," Laurel remarked to the room, in a tone of wonderment.

"And," Weigand said, "somebody with the initials O.M. wrote Merle a note telling him that somebody with the initial L would be at the apartment at about five. To get a check. And Merle went and was killed."

She looked at him for rather a long time before she answered. She drew in a deep breath and her breasts rose pointedly against the silk of her pajamas.

She moistened her lips before she spoke, and when she spoke her voice was less low pitched.

"No, damn it," she said. "It wasn't me. I wasn't anywhere near there. He didn't bring me the check. He—" She broke off. She started over.

"I don't know anything about it," she said. "What do you want me to say?"

What she had said was all right, Weigand told her. If true.

"I'll swear it's true," she said. "Anywhere I'll swear it's true."

"All right," Weigand said. "You weren't at the apartment. You didn't meet Merle—or shoot him. You didn't take the check."

"No," she said. She said it dully. "No."

"Somebody did," Bill Weigand told her. "Somebody met Mr. Merle there and shot him. Somebody took the check. If he brought a check. How well did you know Mr. Merle, Miss Burke?"

She shook her head; for a moment she seemed a long way off. Weigand repeated. "How well did you know Mr. Merle, Miss Burke?"

"Just through Ozzie," she said. She moved slightly. "He came to the apartment a few times to see Ozzie. He knew about Ozzie and me."

She was not speaking dully now. She was speaking carefully—slowly, as if she were thinking it out.

Bill Weigand waited a moment after she had finished. Then he shook his head.

"That's not good enough," he said. "You don't seem to get the situation, Miss Burke. I can take you in as it is—as it is right now. On the basis of the letter. And let you try to work your way out of it. Unless you sell me a better story."

"That's the way it was," the girl said. "Really."

"No," Bill said. "Not unless Ozzie is lying. He says Merle was never at the apartment."

"He—" the girl said. "I don't believe he said that."

"Right," Bill said. "You don't believe he said it. I do. We can take you both down. You can ask him. If you get a chance. We can say you and he were in it together."

Her eyes widened. She stood up suddenly and her voice, too, went up.

"We weren't in anything together," she said. She almost screamed it. "Not in *anything*. You can't make that stick."

Weigand did not meet her mood. His voice was level, casual. He said they could try.

"If Ozzie said that," she said, "it was—it was because he didn't know. He—"

"Didn't know what?" Weigand said. "That Merle was visiting you? While he was paying your apartment rent—while Ozzie was? Is that what Murdock didn't know?"

The girl looked at him and now her eyes were narrow—speculative. She raised her hands and pushed back her hair, which fell in curves around her face. The movement rounded the silk against her body. She let her hands drop and suddenly she shrugged just perceptibly. She sat down again. Her voice regained its studied depth as she spoke.

"Suppose it was," she said. "Suppose—what you want to suppose. Why would I kill him? Suppose I was crossing Ozzie up."

"You were?" Bill said.

"Suppose I was," she said. "Suppose the old boy thought I was—well, thought I was something he wanted. Suppose he made a good bid and I decided a girl's got to live. Would I tell Ozzie everything?"

"Not if Mr. Merle was satisfied with things that way," Bill said. "Was he?"

"He was—suppose he was scared as hell," she said. "Scared people would find out if he—if he got me an honest-to-God place to live. Suppose he wanted me to go on with Ozzie as—as a way to cover up. Suppose he came through with enough—"

"To make it worth your while not to hold out for an honest-to-God place to live. And the rest of it," Bill finished. "Are you saying that was the way it was? A dirty trick on Ozzie?"

"What the hell," the girl said. "You only live once. Is it any of your business?"

"Not that part of it," Bill Weigand told her. "Unless you killed Merle."

"Why would I?" she said. "With things that way I wouldn't have any reason. I'd want to keep him alive. But Ozzie—"

"But Ozzie wouldn't," Weigand said. He looked at her. She was something to look at; but he was no longer even speculatively carnivorous. "So you want to throw us Murdock," he said.

"I'm not throwing you anybody," she told him. "I'm just telling you the way things could have been. Nobody's going to hang it on me. I've got to look after myself."

"You seem to," Weigand told her.

"What the hell," the girl said, "who doesn't?"

Bill Weigand could think of a lot of people who didn't; he could think of casualty lists. But there was no point to it.

"Right," Weigand said. "So this is your story."

He sketched it for her, and as he did so he admitted to himself that it fitted well enough—fitted with the few pieces of the puzzle he had so far found—with Merle's interest in antiques, for example, counting that interest as another cautious blind; it fitted, perhaps, with Merle's character, assuming—as more or less Weigand did assume—that Merle's public austerity was privately superficial. If he had been aroused by Laurel Burke, however frostily, he would go to lengths to keep it quiet. He would, perhaps, accept a situation which might have depressed a more forthright man. And it was, at least in theory, possible that Oscar Murdock, if he found out about it, might not be so complacent. That was so far only a theory, unsupported by facts.

"I don't say Ozzie shot him," the girl said, when Weigand finished. "I just say he might have had a reason—if he found out about us. He never said he found out."

"But if he found out, you think he might have done it?" Weigand said. He looked at her after he had spoken.

"You don't think I'm worth it?" she said, unexpectedly. Consciously, she raised her arms, clasping her hands behind her head. She looked back at Weigand. Her look was a challenge.

Bill Weigand smiled, without amusement.

"I wouldn't know," he said. "I really wouldn't know." He looked into her challenging eyes. "And, baby, I'm not going to try to find out," he added. "So you can quit stretching."

Without violence, Laurel Burke told Weigand what he was. When she had finished, he laughed at her. She started up and then, as quickly, dropped back on the sofa.

"What the hell," she said. "You wouldn't be worth the trouble."

Weigand sat for a moment, looking at her. Then he stood up.

"I don't know," he said, "whether I'm going to buy your story or not. It's a very pretty little story. I can still think of other little stories—not so pretty. Or just about as pretty. So I wouldn't try to go anywhere, if I were you."

"You'll be back, Lieutenant?" she said.

Somebody would be back, he promised her. He would be—or someone else would be.

"So just wait around," he suggested. "Just wait around."

• 7 •

TUESDAY, 10:15 P.M. TO 10:45 P.M.

Pam and Jerry North had had a story to tell Bill Weigand and no Weigand to tell it to. Weigand was not at his office; Mullins had been dispirited on the telephone. He had even been plaintive.

"Yeah," Mullins said. "Yeah. I know. Sure, Mr. North. All I can say is, you oughta of heard the inspector." Mullins sighed, remembering. "I tell you how it is, Mr. North," Mullins went on, his sigh completed. "The inspector knows who did it, like he always does. The loot don't know so easy, like he usually don't. The inspector thinks that's because of you and Mrs. North. And all I can say is, you oughta of heard him."

"He," Jerry said, "oughta to hear us. Or Bill ought. All I want to know, Sergeant, is—where's Bill."

"You'll send me to Staten Island," Mullins said. "Or Rockaway. On foot."

"Do you know where he is?" Jerry wanted to know.

Mullins sighed.

"Well," he said, "in a manner of speaking. I don't know where he is now, Mr. North. I know where he was. He was talking to a dame named Laurel Burke, who he thinks maybe killed Merle. He's going to talk to a guy who maybe killed Merle if Laurel didn't. He just called in. When he called in he was in a drug store."

72

"I—" said Jerry. "All right, Pam. You try."

"Listen, Mr. North," Mullins said. "Listen!"

"Sergeant," Mrs. North said, "we want to know where Bill is. It's important."

"Staten Island," Mullins said. "Or Rockaway. Or even Jamaica. Listen, Mrs. North."

"If you don't you certainly will," Mrs. North said. "Because you'll be obstructing justice. Anyway, in its early stages. And anyway, Jerry can get you a job. Jerry, don't! He's nudging me, Sergeant. But really he would, instead of a place like Jamaica. So you may as well tell us."

"Listen," Mullins said. "I can't do that, Mrs. North. The inspector wouldn't like it. If the loot's going to see this guy Murdock at the Hotel Main on account of maybe he shot the old boy, the inspector don't want you in on it. That's what the inspector says. He says you make it screwy."

"Main?" Pam said. "M-A-I-N?"

"Yeah," Mullins said. "The inspector wants you to stay away from there."

"Thank you, Sergeant," Pam said.

"Absolutely," Mullins said. "Like I was telling the inspector's secretary, who just came in, I can't tell you where Weigand is. And wouldn't if I could, Mrs. North."

"Of course not, Mullins," Mrs. North said. "I wouldn't want you to."

Mr. and Mrs. North caught a taxicab almost at once. They got Murdock's room number by the simple device of asking for it on the Main's house phone and they went up unannounced because, as Mrs. North said, the police department was acting rather odd about them at the moment and it was really important to tell Bill about Mary Hunter, née Thorgson. And since the door of Murdock's room was already a little ajar, Pam, who was ahead, knocked on it only as a formality before she opened it.

It opened on a tiny hallway, with a bath on one side and a closet on the other, and Pam spoke as she preceded Jerry through the hallway into the room. She said: "Bill?"

Nobody answered and, before Jerry was far enough along to see what she saw, she said, "Oh" in a strange voice and drew back against him—drew back into his arms. When he saw what she was looking at, he held her there a moment.

Even if his name had been Bill, instead of Oscar Murdock, the man would not have answered Pam. He was sitting in a chair facing them, and he had slid down in the chair and his right arm dangled. Almost mathematically in the middle of his forehead there was an ugly blur of blood. Blood had run down over his face and down his neck to his shirt. And it was still running.

Under his relaxed right hand a revolver lay on the floor.

They were still looking at the body of Oscar Murdock, who had done confidential work for George Merle and might now be assumed to have hastened after his late employer, when the telephone in the room rang. It rang sharply, hurriedly. At the sound, Pam started convulsively in Jerry's arms.

"O.K., child," Jerry said. "Hold it."

"Answer it, Jerry," Pam said. "It's a clue. It's always a clue when the phone rings."

Jerry hesitated only a moment. Then he stepped around Pam, drawing a handkerchief from his pocket. He picked up the telephone in the handkerchief and said, "Hello?"

He listened a moment, said, "Yes," once, and then said, again: "Hello? Hello?" He put the telephone back in its stand.

"Well," he said.

"Was it a clue?" Pam wanted to know.

Jerry thought a moment and nodded. Probably, he said, it was a clue.

"It was somebody named Laurel," he said. "A girl named Laurel. She said: 'Ozzie! This is Laurel. There's a detective coming over. I had to tell him about Merle but I didn't—' and then she seemed to realize there was something wrong with my voice—that it wasn't Ozzie's. Because she said: 'Ozzie! Is there something—Ozzie!' I said 'Yes' and she made a funny sort of sound and hung up. Does it sound like a clue to you?"

Pam was looking at the body.

"Yes," she said. "Oh, yes. Or anyway it would but—well, I don't know what we'll do with it, do you? Now that Mr. Murdock's killed himself. I suppose because he killed Mr. Merle. So now we've got a solution and we don't need a clue."

They were thinking about that, and Jerry had an arm protectively about Pam's shoulders, when Bill Weigand opened the door behind them. Bill looked at them and at the body.

"It looks," Bill said, "as if I was a little late. Quite a little late."

Bill Weigand went on into the room and bent over the body, not touching it.

"About fifteen minutes late," he said. He looked at Pam and Jerry and raised polite eyebrows. "And you?" he said.

"About twelve minutes," Jerry North told him. "But in time to get a telephone call."

Bill said, "Um-m-m?" and waited. Jerry told him about the call. Bill's eyebrows went up again.

"Laurel Burke," he said. "She sells him out. Then she warns him. Or tries to. 'I had to tell him about Merle but I didn't—'" He shook his head. "And that was all?" he said. Jerry nodded.

"But she didn't tell me something else," Bill said, thinking about it. "About several other things." He looked at the body. "However," he said in a different tone. It was a final tone.

"Apparently," Pam said, "he didn't need a warning, Bill. Were you coming to—to pick him up?"

Bill shook his head, abstractedly. As a matter of fact, he said, he hadn't been. He had still been a good way from that. He had a few questions to ask Murdock—a few new questions. He looked at the body again and shook his head.

"To be honest," he said, "I didn't think he was—it. He knew something. The Burke girl pushed him at me—and gave him a motive. All for the love of Laurel Burke, she had it."

"Of course," Pam said, "you realize you don't make sense. Not to us."

"Well," Bill said. "Sauce for the goose. The Burke girl says her heart belonged to Mr. Merle and that poor Ozzie was just camouflage. She suggests Ozzie found out and didn't like the setup. Whereupon, bang! Do you like it?"

"Not terribly," Jerry North said. "Nice and simple, however. And—" He gestured toward the body of Oscar Murdock. Weigand nodded.

"Right," he said. "Whether we like it or not. There it is—all nice and clear for us. Murdock killed Merle. He decided he wasn't going to get away with it. Maybe I scared him earlier. So he decided to finish the story himself—in private. Instead of in a bright room, with a lot of witnesses. Neater, he probably thought."

Pam said, with something like a shudder, that "neat" was an odd word for it. Bill pointed out that Murdock hadn't been thinking about people who came in afterward. For him, it was neat enough. One shot in the forehead and—. Bill shrugged without finishing. He picked up the telephone, not bothering to cover it against prints. He called the number of the Homicide office; asked curtly for Inspector O'Malley. He outlined the story briefly. He listened, said, "Yes, Inspector," and "No, Inspector," half a dozen times and hung up. He turned from the telephone and said the boys would be along. To take care of formalities.

Pam was looking at the body, fixedly. Bill stepped between her and the body just as Jerry put a hand on her shoulder.

"Forget it, kid," Jerry said. "You'll be dreaming about it."

Pam shook her head.

"It isn't that," she said. "But isn't it a funny place? Awkward? The wound, I mean."

Bill turned and looked at the body and turned back, shaking his head a little.

"Not particularly," he said. "You mean it ought to be in the side of the head?"

Pam nodded.

"There's no rule about it," Bill Weigand said. "I see what you mean, but there's no rule about it. There are—different ways."

"Still," Pam insisted, "it would be awkward. You'd have to hold the gun out in front of you and turn it in and—. It would be awkward."

"You could turn your head to meet the gun," Jerry pointed out. "Or—or pull the trigger with your thumb. It wouldn't be particularly difficult."

Pam nodded, but without conviction.

"I know," she said. "I see how it could be done. I don't mean it isn't possible—or even that it would be terribly hard. But I'd think that—that you'd want to do it as easily as possible. Mechanically, I mean. With as little wrestling around and—"

She was still looking at the body when she stopped speaking. She was looking at it with a new intentness.

"Particularly," she said, "if you had a wrist like Murdock's. A wrist which wouldn't bend easily. Look at it."

Bill stepped forward and squatted to look closely at the dangling right hand. After a moment, he touched it lightly. He stood up, unconsciously wiping his fingers on his handkerchief. He looked puzzled.

"Would it?" Pam said.

Slowly, Bill shook his head.

"Some time or other," he said, "Murdock had a broken wrist. It wasn't set quite properly—it's what they call a silver-fork deformity. He had practically full use of it, probably, and the malformation isn't very visible. But—"

"But," Pam said, "he couldn't bend it the normal distance forward, could he, Bill?" She turned to Jerry quickly. "You remember Cousin Willard, Jerry?"

"Vividly," Jerry said.

"All right," Pam said. "Anyway you like—at the moment. He had a wrist like that. He broke it cranking a car. A Chevrolet. The battery didn't work. And he couldn't make it go forward properly."

"Not even by crank—" Jerry began and stopped. "Oh," he said. "I see what you mean. The wrist. Not the Chevrolet."

Pam said, "Of course.

"And," she said, "to hold a revolver up against the middle of your forehead the way Murdock did, you'd have to have your wrist go forward—your hand go forward, I mean. At right angles to your arm. And Willard's wouldn't."

The two men looked at each other. After a moment, Jerry half smiled.

"Even if you moved your head toward the gun," he said. "It would be possible, I suppose. But it would be—well, Pam's word fits, Bill. Awkward."

Bill nodded slowly.

"Damned awkward," he said. He smiled, not cheerfully. "In more ways than one," he said. "I just told the inspector Murdock had finished himself off and saved us the trouble. He won't like it if Murdock didn't. Particularly if—."

He reached quickly for the telephone; talked quickly into it. Then he talked more slowly and listened longer. A rumbling noise, to which the Norths paid careful inattention, came from the receiver. After a considerable time, and as there was a firm knock on the door, Weigand put the telephone back in its cradle.

"He's already told the reporters," Bill said, sadly. "He doesn't like it at all. All right, boys."

The boys came. They came with cameras and fingerprint blanks and a general air of competence. A hospital intern came with them, looked at the body from a distance, said, "D.O.A.," and wrote the same in a notebook and went away. The men of the Homicide Squad moved around the room, not touching the body. Flashbulbs flared and cameras peered down at angles on the body of Oscar Murdock. An assistant medical examiner came with a black bag, looked the body over without opening the bag, said they could send it along.

"Looks like suicide," he said, contentedly.

"Doesn't it?" Bill Weigand said, without content.

The Homicide fingerprint men took over the body. They rolled the fingers one by one on a pad and on numbered slips of paper.

"Of course," Jerry said, "he could have used his thumb. Or his left hand."

"Right," Bill said. "Or his big toe. If he used his left hand, why did he drop the gun with his right? And the prints aren't going to show he used his thumb."

Bill Weigand was morose.

"Look, Bill," Pam North said. "It isn't—well, conclusive. He *could* have done it."

"Right," Bill said. "He *could* have done it—just like that. And somebody could have done it for him—held the revolver close to his head and pulled the trigger; bent his hand around the gun after wiping it. Not noticing Murdock's wrist. And when we catch him, *he'll* say Murdock *could* have done it, wrist or no wrist, and the doctors will have to say sure, he could have—it wasn't physically impossible. It just wasn't likely. And the jury will probably decide that that means a reasonable doubt and—the hell with it!"

"Look, Bill," Pam said. "You make it sound awful. I'm sorry. I didn't mean to—to—what does Mullins say? Make it screwy. I just happened to notice."

Bill grinned at her.

"Oh," he said, "the truth above everything, Pam. Even if inconvenient. Only I wish you'd happened to notice before I called Art—Inspector O'Malley. However."

There was a pause, while they watched the busy men from Homicide.

"Now what?" Pam said.

"Now," Jerry said, "you and I go home. Bill—what do you do, Bill?"

Bill shook his head, abstractedly.

"I," he said, "spread it out and look at it. At home, I think." He paused. "Tell you," he said, "why don't you and Pam drop around. We'll give you a drink. We'll put your little minds to work, too, probably. And we won't tell the inspector, huh?"

Pam looked suddenly surprised.

"Of course," she said. "We've got to. That's why we came here in the first place, Bill. To get you so we could tell you why Mary Hunter hated Mr. Merle. And this—this put it out of our heads. Didn't it, Jerry?"

TUESDAY, 10:45 P.M. TO WEDNESDAY, JUNE 14, 12:35 A.M.

The early editions of the tabloids were full of the story. The *Mirror* thought it more important than the war and its front page blared: "Banker Slain in Girl's Flat!" The *News* had had, one could suspect, a short, unhappy struggle with its conscience. War remained dominant. But the untimely death of George Merle captured the third page and was complete with diagram, including an outline drawing of Merle's sprawled body. It was the body of a man, and it was clothed, but it was after all a body. There was an inset cut of Mary Hunter and in the caption the *News* asked itself a question. "Why," the *News* inquired, "did millionaire banker visit pretty widow of Naval hero?" The *News* did not reply, but it managed to smirk slightly. There, its story indicated— its story in double column, with appropriately double authorship— there was a question it could answer, and it would.

But whatever lay between the lines, the lines themselves were irreproachable and naive. Mr. Merle had been a banker of great wealth and, as was natural under circumstances so auspicious, almost notorious probity. He was indefatigable in good works; he was at once devout and philanthropic, as much vestryman as company director. It was inconceivable that anyone could have wished him ill and, so wishing him, planted three .38 calibre slugs in his chest. The *News* was chagrined at what the world was coming to, even while it gloated over what had come to Page 3. It had even managed a hurried editorial in which, with the dexterity of long practice, it indicated without precisely saying so—without, indeed, precisely saying anything whatever—that the tragedy reported on Page 3 was only what one could expect in a country which, for three Presidential terms, had seethed with deliberately fanned class hatred. "Is This A Warning?" the *News* asked itself, editorially. It seemed to the *News* that probably it was.

The Norths scanned the papers as the Buick, sedate now and obedient to traffic signals, ambled toward the Weigand apartment in the Murray Hill district. They scanned them in glimpses under street lights, and they read Bill Weigand excerpts from time to time. Between excerpts, Bill switched the radio to the broadcast band and a bell rang. The *Times* told in measured sentences of the world at war. At the end it admitted a minor note. "The police have just announced," the *Times* said, "the suicide of Oscar Murdock, business associate of the late George Merle, who was questioned earlier this evening in connection with Mr. Merle's murder this afternoon in a Madison Avenue apartment." The *Times* did not amplify and returned to the headline war news for the benefit of any who, not punctual to his hourly rendezvous with history, might have tuned in late. The *Times* let the implications lie as they would, which was heavily.

Weigand stopped the Buick in front of the apartment and flicked off the radio. He sat for a moment, a little wrinkle in his forehead, and then moved quickly. He led the Norths into the building and the elevator; he led them into his own apartment on the fifth floor. He did not even pause for more than a smile at Dorian, looking up suddenly from the drawing pad in her lap, turning suddenly in her chair as Pam North said something to Jerry—something to indicate presence on the scene and the intrusion of outsiders. Pam North deeply believed, not without evidence, that there was no telling what married people would say to each other when they thought they were alone. She remembered one time—She put the memory back in safe-keeping and thought of other things.

Bill was at the telephone. Already he was talking crisply to Deputy

Chief Inspector Artemus O'Malley. The crispness showed through the politeness.

"Right," he said. "Then you haven't told them different? It's still suicide?" He waited. "I know, Inspector," he said. "I know. Yes, I should have. Yes." He waited again. "The point is," he said, "why not play it that way, now that we've gone this far? It will get the story out of our hair for a day or two. It looks as if we were supposed to think it was suicide. It looks—" He broke off, listening. His face looked tired. But when he managed to get in again his voice was not tired.

"Right," he said. "But here's what I'd like to do, with the things the way they are. Let the killer think he's fooled us. Let him think he's pinned it on Murdock. Let him have his little laugh. Maybe he'll be laughing so hard he won't see us coming. And then we tell the newspaper boys sure, we planned it that way right along—a sp—a trap to catch woodcocks."

He paused and listened. He smiled slightly.

"I know," he said. "They'll burrow under anything, Inspector." He listened further. "That's tough," he said. "All of it? That's sure tough." He made faces over the telephone at the other three. His face straightened. "No," he said, "they haven't got much to do with it, Inspector." The inspector rumbled.

"Right," he said. "I think you've got something there, Inspector. We'll let it ride along as is for a while, anyway. And meantime I'll keep on it. Right?" The telephone rumbled. "Right," Bill said. He put the telephone down and looked at it. He looked up from it at his wife and the Norths.

"The inspector thinks we'd better not tell the press it wasn't suicide," he reported gravely. "The inspector's got an idea there's no use telling the killer how much we know." He barely smiled. "He also," he added, "thinks woodcocks are woodchucks. They've been eating his broccoli. How are all the pretty pictures?"

The last was to Dorian Weigand. She showed him pretty pictures of tall girls in new clothes, pictures of tall girls in new clothes being Dorian Weigand's occupation. Bill Weigand smiled at them blissfully, as one might smile at genius. Dorian looked over his bent head, her lips curled in a smile, her greenish eyes lively under long lashes.

"*I,*" she said. "Think he's sweet. Don't you? He thinks I'm—oh, Cézanne."

Bill took hold of her head, ostensibly by the ears. He shook it slightly and let it go.

"Why not?" he said. "You think I'm Sherlock." He looked at her. "I hope," he added.

Pam North turned to Jerry.

"Dr. Watson, I presume," she said.

Jerry agreed solemnly.

"Of course, Mrs. Watson," he said. "Fancy meeting us here."

"I'll get you drinks," Dorian promised, pushing Bill back so she could stand up. She walked across the room toward the kitchen and Bill looked at her with admiration. He looked at the Norths and did not hide his admiration. They smiled at him, agreeing. Nobody said anything. They sat down in familiar chairs and, by unspoken agreement, did not begin until Dorian came back with a tray. It was a big tray and she was not big, but she carried it easily, with grace. She mixed without orders, calling off—Pam, a little rye and lots of water; Jerry, some scotch and not so much water; Bill, scotch and soda. "Me, scotch and soda too, like Bill." She smiled at him.

"It was because he wouldn't let her marry Josh," Pam said, beginning in the middle. "Or Josh marry her, which is the same thing, of course. Because he hated her father, but she doesn't know why. Mary Hunter, I mean."

"What was because of that, Pam?" Bill asked her, and Dorian looked from one to another, her eyes wide.

"That was why she said, she said he ought to die," Pam explained. "That's why she's so frightened. Because she said that to him, and then he did die. In her apartment."

Bill looked interested. He said, "Oh?" and looked at Jerry North. Jerry reached across the little space between their chairs and captured one of Pam's hands. He said to let him tell it; let him, anyway, put a foundation under it. He told Dorian and Bill about the interview in the big house on Long Island between a slight girl in white and an implacable man behind a heavy desk. He told what had led up to that interview, as far as they knew it, and what came after.

"She left after she said that—that about thinking George Merle ought to die," he said. "She left without seeing Josh Merle. She went home and waited for him to call—waited for him to tell her it didn't matter what his father said or what his father did—that nothing and nobody could stop their getting married. Only—well, the kid didn't call. He didn't call that night or the next day—he just never did call."

"And so," Pam said, "she decided he cared most about the money and she wrote him a letter—one letter—saying—well, saying he cared most about the money. And he didn't answer that. And that winter he went into the Navy as an aviation cadet after Pearl Harbor and quite a while later Mary met Rick Hunter and married him and he went off and got killed. Only I think she loved Josh all the time, except that of course she hated him too. And she hated his father, I guess."

Bill sat thinking it over, his face remote.

"He just—dropped her?" he said. "When papa said no more dough? Just like that—is that what you gathered?"

"Just like that," Jerry told him.

"Of course," Pam said, "it doesn't mean they didn't meet again—things like that. I mean—oh, neither of them was walled up, or anything. They both kept on going around. I gather they met but—but not to talk to each other. Not really to talk."

"And if he had a side of it?" Bill said. "Just to get it straight."

"What side?" Pam wanted to know.

Bill Weigand shrugged slightly. He pointed out that they didn't know what Josh Merle's father might have told Josh.

"You make it sound—oh, like the cruel parent in something or other," Pam said.

So, Bill pointed out, did she. And, he added, cruel parents sometimes got killed. In stories.

"And for that matter," he added, "out of stories."

"For revenge?" Pam said. "Really, Bill."

"Even for revenge," Bill told her. "For all kinds of reasons, people kill. But I wasn't thinking of that—or, at any rate, not primarily of that. You could work it out another way."

"Could you?" Jerry said. "I don't—." He broke off. He broke off because Pam was looking at him and shaking her head.

"Oh, yes, Jerry," she said. "Oh, yes you could. We may as well admit it, even if it isn't true. Because now she's a widow."

Jerry said, "Oh."

"Right," Bill said. "Now she's a widow—now she could marry Josh. God, what a name!"

Pam shook her head at him. She said lots of people had it.

"Only," she said, "maybe not people you fall in love with much. I'll give you that. And get the money."

"Right," Bill said, and was faintly surprised at his readily understanding. "Suppose she thought she could hit it off with Josh again, now that she was—older—more experienced. And free again. Suppose she—well, loved him in a fashion, wanted to prove to herself that she couldn't just be ditched—and wanted money. And the only thing in the way would be the boy's father. And now—well, now he isn't in the way. And now he can't cut Josh off with—what is it?—a shilling. Now Josh won't have to choose between her and the money. He can have both. As, taking it the other way, so can she. Which gives her a motive."

"And," Pam pointed out, "him. Two fine motives. But why the other man with the funny name—Oswald something? Why kill him?"

"Because," Bill said, "Oscar—not Oswald—Murdock knew something. That made a good enough reason."

"Or," Jerry suggested, "because it was convenient."

The others waited. Jerry's voice was faintly doubtful as he amplified.

"Suppose," he said, "that the murderer knew Murdock was under suspicion. He was, wasn't he?"

Bill Weigand thought it over. He agreed you might call it that.

"Vague suspicion," he said. "And chiefly after I had talked to his girl—Laurel. Before that I was just—call it—curious."

"All right," Jerry said. "Call it merely curious. But the murderer didn't need to know that. He might have thought you were—oh, hot on his trail. Baying at his heels."

"He doesn't," Dorian said firmly. "Did you ever hear him, Pam?"

Bill shook his head at her. He nodded it at Jerry.

"And," Jerry went on, "decide that Murdock was made to order as a fall guy. Suspected by the police, Murdock kills himself. Neater, that way. The chase is ended. The case is solved. The police forget the whole thing. The murderer sleeps soundly of nights." Jerry paused and thought it over. "Actually," he added, "I think that's one of our better motives. Straightforward, simple—you kill one man; you arrange for another man to kill himself—to appear to kill himself—under circumstances which will lead the police, notoriously unbright, to accept suicide as confession."

"And," Bill Weigand agreed dryly, "the police live up to their bill. And the amateur saves the day."

"Seriously," Pam said, "seriously, I rather like it."

Bill Weigand nodded slowly. He said he didn't dislike it.

"And," he said, "we have no evidence one way or the other. When we catch the man who killed Merle, we can always ask him why he killed Murdock. But merely guessing at the *reason* for Murdock's murder doesn't seem to get us anywhere."

It would. Pam North pointed out, if they knew enough about character. If they knew who would think like that.

"Besides Jerry, of course," she said. "Jerry doesn't count. He was with me." She considered that. "Anyway," she said, "when Murdock was killed."

Bill said they should try to keep it simple—keep it, anyway, simpler than that. Because, he said, they didn't know enough about character—about the way people were, how they thought, what they would do.

"Because," he said, "it comes down to guesswork—to guessing what we would do if we were in the position some one else is in. We think he would do a certain thing, for a certain reason—meaning that *we* think *we* would do that thing for that reason in his place. But we're not even sure, most of the time, what *we* would do. And our guesses about other people—even people we know very well—well, they aren't good enough."

"I can guess what you will do," Dorian told him. "At least, most of the time."

He looked at her, and smiled. He said he hoped she could; he said he thought she could. Most of the time. As, he said, Pam could guess what Jerry could do and Jerry could guess—. He stopped at that, overcome by doubt.

"The funny thing," Pam said, "is that he can. Even sometimes when I can't. It's disconcerting sometimes. Like eternal recurrence."

Everybody looked at her.

"Probably," Jerry said, "she means predestination. It makes her feel hemmed in, as if she had to do what I think she's going to do."

Pam said she thought "recurrence" was better. Just going around and around, over and over again, and people catching you as you came by. She said she wasn't sure it wasn't that way, but she hoped not. Although sometimes Jerry frightened her.

"But just as often," she said, "he seems to be surprised, even by the simplest things. However, I don't see where this gets us, because we're talking about me instead of the murderer. It's nice, of course, but it isn't really very—very practical."

There was a slight pause. Pam broke it.

"What we ought to decide," she said, "is who have we got?"

Bill Weigand held his left hand up in front of him, and seemed to be looking at his nails. Slowly he pulled down the thumb with the index finger of his right hand.

"Mary Hunter," he said. "To get Joshua and the money." He pulled down the index finger of his left hand. "Joshua Merle," he said. "To get Mary and the money. He rubbed his left thumb and index finger together. "Or both of them," he said. "Like that." He pulled down the finger next in line. He said, "Laurel Burke."

The others looked at him in surprise. Jerry, after a moment of thought, said he thought Laurel Burke was out. On a time basis, if nothing else. Weigand shook his head.

"I stopped on the way to make some telephone calls," he said. "It may have taken me—oh, ten minutes. And I didn't drive fast, particularly. And when I left I took off the man who had been keeping an eye on her. If she left at once, got a cab and did drive fast, she might have been at Murdock's room ten minutes before I got there—possibly twelve minutes. Five or seven minutes before you two got there. She kills him and gets out—the killing takes a couple of minutes, including setting the stage for suicide. It wasn't an elaborate stage setting. She goes downstairs and sees you come in. When she's sure you're in Murdock's room she calls and pretends that she thinks Murdock is still alive and that she wants to warn him."

"Why?" Pam said.

"Why which," Bill said. "Why murder? Why pretend?"

"Both," Pam said. "Or either."

As for the first, Bill Weigand said, Jerry's theory fitted very nicely. Because Laurel Burke had made what might have been a deliberate effort to throw suspicion on Murdock. Possibly she was getting Weigand's mind ready for confession by suicide. Why the pretense she thought Murdock still alive? Obviously because it looked good—made her appear innocent. As a matter of fact, she had identified herself, by name. Which one might think wouldn't be necessary, since she and Murdock obviously knew each other very well indeed, and might be expected to know each other's voices. One might think, indeed, that she would be able to tell Jerry North's voice from Murdock's as soon as Jerry answered the telephone.

"Look," Pam said, "maybe she *did* do it."

"Maybe," Weigand agreed. He added that it would help to know why she had killed Merle, since they were assuming that whoever killed Murdock killed Merle—and had an original reason to kill Merle, rather than Murdock. He paused and smiled faintly.

"Of course," he said, "we could make it even more intricate, if we wanted to. Suppose the whole thing was set up to kill Murdock—to give Murdock a reason for suicide so that murder would be accepted as suicide. In that event, Merle isn't a victim, exactly—really, Merle is a motive."

"That," Pam said, "is worse than anything I ever thought up. Much worse. As a motive for murder—well—."

Bill Weigand smiled slightly and admitted he wasn't betting on it.

But he added that motives were, at the best, odd things—what was a motive for one person wasn't a motive for another. What would hardly irritate one person would lead another to murder—and murder the hard way. Money was a simple motive—but the amount of money was unpredictable. Murder had happened for a few dollars; a gang of men had once spent weeks murdering a strangely resistant vagrant for five hundred dollars of insurance money. And a doctor had once been accused of trying to murder quite a large family so that his wife would inherit the family money—and not very much money. Men had killed other men who laughed at them, or who threatened to make them so ridiculous that others would laugh. It was difficult to think of any motive which would persuade some people to murder; an almost imperceptible flick to self-esteem or self-interest might turn other people into killers. That was academic—he was not prepared to argue, at least not for very long, that Merle had been killed to set the stage for the primary murder of Oscar Murdock.

But they could, if they went to a little trouble, easily suppose a motive for Laurel Burke's murder of the banker—as a primary murder. There might be any number of motives hidden in the relationships between Laurel, Merle and Murdock—hidden because they knew so far only as much of those relationships as Laurel and, to a lesser degree, Murdock himself, had let drop. Even what they knew or could guess at would supply a motive of sorts.

"Suppose," he said, "that she was shaking Merle down—with or without Murdock's aid. Suppose Merle went there to see her and she went to meet him, expecting a payoff. But suppose he didn't pay—suppose, instead, he threatened her. Suppose he threatened her with the police. Or, if Murdock wasn't in it, suppose he threatened her with Murdock. She's a fairly violent b—girl. Maybe she got mad and began pulling the trigger. Suppose she shot Murdock because he knew she was there—maybe he knew she was going there, maybe he happened to come in in time to catch her, or just happened to be passing and saw her leave."

Jerry was shaking his head.

"The trouble with all this is," he said, "that the Murdocks didn't live there any more—either Murdock. Mary Hunter lived there. And Murdock knew it because he had rented her the apartment."

Bill nodded and said that was a catch. He said that was another thing about which they didn't know enough. At the moment, it was evidently an argument that Murdock had not written the note which apparently took Merle to the apartment. It was also an argument against Laurel Burke's being in the apartment, because she, presumably, also knew it had been rented. At least she knew she had moved out. They would know more about that when—and if—they found the typewriter on which the note had been typed. That would take time.

"For one thing," he pointed out—"for one nice initial complication—it could be practically any typewriter at the Madison Avenue Bank and Trust Company. Murdock would have had access there—he could have given access to Laurel. Joshua Merle could have used a typewriter there if he'd wanted."

Bill stopped and looked sad.

"And so," he said, "could probably hundreds of other people. So it will use up time. And there is no particular reason to think that the typewriter is in the bank at all."

He sighed. He looked at the fingers he still held up. He drew down another. And another. And another.

"The antique man," he said. "Because he was annoyed at Merle for not buying the chair. Because Merle knew he made artificial antiques and threatened to expose him."

"Did he?" Pam said.

Bill nodded.

"The elevator man," he said. "Who rather oddly didn't hear Mary Hunter scream—if she did scream. Weldon Jameson."

"Who—?" Dorian said a little helplessly. "People keep coming in."

Josh's friend, Bill Weigand explained. A good-looking youngster a couple of years younger than Joshua Merle; apparently a devoted friend; apparently, like Merle, a washed-out flyer who had cracked up in an accident of some sort. What sort—and what the two young men had done in the Navy generally—was being looked up.

"Why?" Pam wanted to know.

Bill shrugged.

"Do you," he said, "want me to run up a motive? I could, I suppose. Arbitrarily—I haven't evidence to indicate *any* motive. Maybe he wanted to give his friend a hand up—get him the money and the girl. Maybe old Merle had done something else he didn't like—you see, we haven't anything to go on."

"Or," Pam said, "any place to go, I shouldn't think. In that direction. How about Mary's father—Mr.—what was his name, Jerry?"

"Thorgson," Jerry said. "Why?"

"Because," Pam said, "Merle had done him out of some money somehow. Which was why Merle hated him and wouldn't let his daughter marry his son. Damn!" She stopped and they looked at her. "Relatives," she said. "Not people relatives—pronoun relatives. Wouldn't let Thorgson's daughter marry his, Merle's son. And so Thorgson murdered Merle."

"Except," Jerry said mildly, "except for one thing, Pam, that sounds fine. The thing is—Thorgson's dead. Isn't he?"

Pam said, "Oh."

"Oh, of course," she said. "I could have liked him—as a murderer, I mean. Is there anybody else?"

"Probably," Bill said. "Hundreds, probably. Persons unknown—persons I'll meet tomorrow on Long Island when I go to have a look around. Persons—"

The telephone rang. Bill Weigand answered it. He listened, said, "Right" and, after another moment, "Thanks." He hung up.

"Well," he said, "he didn't use his thumb. The print on the trigger—what there was of it—was of his right index finger. He was shot with the same gun used to kill Merle. Ballistics is sure of that. And the doc agrees that his right wrist was stiff from an old fracture, not very well set. Stiff enough so that it would have been awkward—but not impossible—for him to hold the gun in position to put a bullet into his own forehead. It wasn't a contact wound, incidentally—the gun was held off maybe a foot. Which makes it look pretty much the way we thought it looked."

For a few minutes nobody said anything. Then Pam said that, in a way, it was a pity, because it made things so much harder. Bill

Weigand said she didn't know how much harder, and when the others waited for him to go on he amplified.

"Because," he said, "it's easier to be pretty sure we're right than to prove we're right. We've got an improbability. But we haven't any more than that. Can you see what a defense attorney will do with it? Why do we insist that it was his client, not Murdock, who killed Merle? Why do we say Murdock didn't kill himself when the going got tough? Because he had a stiff wrist. Oh, so he couldn't have shot himself, is that it? It was physically impossible? Well, no. Oh, so you admit it wasn't impossible? Then why do you decide he *didn't* kill himself? Well, it would have been awkward. It would have been inconvenient. And then our defense lawyer throws up his hands and does double takes for the jury and what does the jury do?"

"The jury," Pam North said, "decides it was Murdock after all, because what is convenience when you're going to kill yourself? Although, as a matter of fact, I'd think it was a lot. If I were going to do it, I'd want to do it just as conveniently as possible. I'd think that awkwardness just then would be—well, almost more important than awkwardness at any other time. Because it would be so—so trivial. So anti-climactic. But would a jury?"

Nobody answered her and when, after a pause, she spoke again it was on quite a different subject.

"What I wonder is," she said, "who got the check? The check that Mr. Merle took to the apartment?"

Maybe, Jerry suggested, he didn't take it. Maybe that was why he got shot. Maybe the absence of the check annoyed someone. Or maybe the murderer got it and just tore it up. Pam shook her head at that. She said she had once and it had been dreadful, because it made the bank so mad. She said she had had an argument about whether she had given or sold something to someone and when the other person had insisted she had torn up the check.

"And the bank was mad," she said. "It was mad for years."

They all looked at her doubtfully. Finally Dorian said, mildly, that she didn't see why the bank was mad.

"Because," Pam said, "it upset their bookkeeping."

Jerry ran a hand through his hair.

"Listen, Pam," he said. "It wouldn't. It wouldn't possibly. A check is just a piece of paper if you tear it up. It couldn't make the bank mad."

"Well," Pam said, "I don't care what you say. It did make the bank mad. They had taken the money out of the account beforehand and so they had to wait because the check might come through and so nobody had the money—not the bank or the person who gave the check or me. It just wasn't anywhere. I'll admit I didn't ever understand it, but that's the way it was. The money just disappeared, somehow. And it was very bad for bookkeeping."

Jerry ran his hand through his hair again.

"But—" he began. Then he stopped and a faraway look came into his eyes. He looked at Bill and Bill began to nod.

"Listen, Pam," Jerry said. "I almost hate to ask this, but—was it a certified check?"

Pam said oh yes, it was certified all right. She said that that was one of the things the bank kept saying over and over. The bank kept saying over and over, "but it was a *certified* check. People don't tear up *certified* checks."

"Which," Pam added, "was nonsense. Because as I kept telling *them* over and over, I had."

· 9 ·

WEDNESDAY, 9:20 A.M. TO 1:15 P.M.

The late editions of the morning newspapers had noticeably lost
interest. The *Times* did, to be sure, begin the story on Page 1, but not as
if it were really proud of it. It did run it for two columns, giving a good
deal more detail—including speculative detail about Mary Hunter—
than the tabloids, but the account had a slight air of weariness. The
Times, without saying so, indicated that the case was finished with the
suicide of Murdock. And at the end of the second column, the *Times*
definitely dropped the subject. The *Herald Tribune* retained slightly
more optimism, and fought against its own gloomy conviction that the
case was solved, but it did not fight with confidence. The *News* moved
the story to Page 2 and gave Page 3 back to the war and the iniquities
of the administration. The *Mirror* hinted that there was more to all of it
than met the eye, but its hints were unusually shadowy.

It was all, Bill Weigand decided, as it should be. Always providing
that eventually he got somewhere. He sighed and took up reports. For
the most part they confirmed the already known—the fracture of Murdock's wrist, the index fingerprint on the gun, the identity of the gun
with the one used to kill Merle, the importance of Merle, who, in addition to being a banker, was in the Social Register, was affectionately
mentioned in Dun and Bradstreet and was favorably known to the

financial secretaries of half a dozen accredited charities. He was also, the *Times* noted, a distinguished layman.

"What I could do with," Weigand told Mullins, "is somebody who didn't like him. Somebody who thought he was a heel. I want the Nell he did wrong by. Nobody kills a saint."

Mullins looked puzzled.

"Look, Loot," he said, "that's how they get to be saints. Lots of times. By being killed."

Bill looked at Mullins sharply, uneasily suspecting him of cynicism. Then he smiled. He said he didn't mean real saints—church saints.

"Oh," Mullins said. "O.K., Loot."

Mullins tapped a cigarette out of Weigand's package. He lighted it.

"Like always," he said, when the light was certain, "there're rumors. About girls, mostly. Only not anything you can put a finger on. You say, maybe, that it looks like Mr. Merle was a pretty fine citizen, respectable and everything. And somebody says, 'Yeah, that's how it looks, doesn't it?' in a kinda funny way. Like they were thinking about girls, or maybe that he used to rob the poor box when he had the time. Or you say, 'Did he have any girl friends?' and people say they wouldn't know about that as if they would know about it but ain't saying."

"But," Bill said, "nothing you can pin down?"

Mullins shook his head. He said that was the size of it. Nothing you could pin down.

"Only," he said, "I've been getting the idea that a lot of people didn't like him much. Even if he did own a bank."

Merle hadn't, Bill Weigand pointed out, really owned the bank. Not all of it. He had merely run it. Mullins said that, as far as he could see, that was just as good. Either way, you made out all right. George Merle was an outstanding example of a guy who had made out all right.

"He's *really* got it," Mullins said. "He's going to make the inheritance tax collectors a fine corpse. State *and* Federal."

Bill Weigand said he supposed there wasn't any doubt of that. Mullins said that he hadn't, of course, counted it personally, but if it wasn't there a lot of people were going to be mighty surprised. Including, Mullins said he wouldn't wonder, the guy who bumped him off.

"Or," Mullins added, looking at Lieutenant Weigand to see how he took it, "the girl."

"Or the girl," Bill agreed, without indicating anything by his tone. "Anybody can use a gun. Which girl do you favor, Sergeant?"

Mullins said he hadn't thought of more than one. The girl who lived in the apartment. Weigand explained Laurel Burke-Murdock and Mullins nodded during the explanation, indicating that he would consider her, too. But he said he still thought that if it was a dame, it was the Hunter dame. If it was a guy, it probably was Josh Merle.

"On account of he probably gets the money," Mullins said. "And when rich guys get killed, you look for the guy who gets the money."

"Oh, while we're talking about him," Mullins said, "the Navy came through."

He took a two-page letter out of a brown envelope and tossed it to Weigand. It was "From: Bureau of Naval Personnel, To: Commanding Officer, Homicide Bureau, New York, New York, Police Department." It was "Subject: Cadet Joshua Merle, Service record of" and it was divided by numerals, one, two, three.

Extracted from verbiage, the facts were not complex. Joshua Merle had been a naval aviation cadet until eight months previously, in training as a bomber pilot. He had been separated from the service, honorably, because of injuries received in training.

"Subject cadet," the letter said, "crashed in landing in a twin-motored training plane, sustaining extensive injuries to his right foot, said injuries necessitating his separation from the service. Cadet Weldon Jameson, flying with Merle at the time, was similarly seriously injured, sustaining a fracture of the right knee. Both cadets were separated from the service after treatment failed to render them fit for further active service in the United States Navy."

Weigand read the letter, glanced over it again and tossed it into the "File" basket. He remarked that it didn't say who was piloting the plane at the time of the crash.

"Should it?" Mullins said. "Do we want to know?"

"We want to know everything, don't we, Sergeant?" Bill Weigand inquired, politely. "We leave no stones unturned, Sergeant."

"O.K., Loot," Mullins said, not evidently discomfited. "Do we want to know much?"

Bill Weigand thought it over for a moment. He said he didn't think they wanted to know much. There were, anyway, things they wanted to know more. For one thing, he would like to know more about the way Joshua Merle had spent his afternoon in town—more specifically. He would like to have somebody find some people Joshua Merle had talked to; he would like to know what bars he had visited, and whether any of them remembered his visits. He would like to know when young Merle limped out of the Yale Club. He would like to know why he walked so much.

"Yeah," Mullins said. "With a game foot and all."

"Right," Weigand said.

Mullins sighed and got up. Bill Weigand watched him a moment and then said, "Not you, Mullins. We'll put some of the other boys on it. You and I are going out on Long Island to look around a bit."

Mullins broke a sigh in two. He sat quickly and said, "O.K., Loot," with enthusiasm. Weigand picked up the telephone. When he put it down he had talked to the State Police and arranged for one of the men from the Criminal Identification Department to go with him to the Merle house, lending authority where Weigand, directly, lacked it. He had talked to a lawyer in a small town—but a town with very rich connections—on the North Shore and had arranged to have a look at George Merle's will.

He had talked to Deputy Chief Inspector O'Malley—he had listened to Deputy Chief Inspector O'Malley. Then he had stood up, looked abstractedly at his desk and let his fingers drum on it, and gone rather suddenly to the door.

In the Buick he let Mullins drive. But when Mullins, angling east toward the East River Drive, came to Fourth Avenue, Bill suddenly checked him.

"Uptown," he said. "We may as well go by Mr. Merle's bank."

They went up Fourth and into Park; above Grand Central they turned west to Madison. The bank was a large and dignified one in the Fifties. It had not closed in memory of Mr. Merle; there was no display of crêpe. But the vice president to whom Weigand's inquiries took them was adequately funereal. Pain crossed his face when Mr. Merle was mentioned and he murmured, with evident reverence, some memorial words. Weigand agreed that it was very sad. He nudged the conversation toward facts.

Mr. Merle had come in at a little after ten the day before, in accordance with his custom. He had been in his office until around one, when he had gone out, no doubt to lunch. He had returned before three and remained until almost four thirty.

"Rather later than usual," the vice president said. "He was an example to all of us."

Mullins started to say "Huh?" but Weigand's eyes stopped him. Weigand repeated that it was very sad. He wondered whether he might see Mr. Merle's secretary.

The vice president's face was not a mobile one, but it displayed surprising mobility. He looked at Weigand with eyes, which, in the face of a lesser man, would have expressed astonishment.

"But—" he said and stopped. He tried it again.

"But, Lieutenant," he said. "Mr. Murdock is—is dead. He—he died. I thought—that is, I understood—I mean—."

"Right," Bill said, smiling faintly. "I hadn't realized that Mr. Murdock was Mr. Merle's secretary. I am quite aware that Mr. Murdock is dead, as the newspapers say. But didn't Mr. Merle have another secretary? A—I don't know what you would call it. A stenographic secretary?"

"Oh," the vice president said. "You mean Miss Werty?"

"Miss?" Weigand said. "Oh, yes—no doubt I mean Miss Werty. I wonder whether I might see Miss Werty?"

He could. He did. Miss Werty appeared, with notebook. Miss Werty was thin and dark and constricted. Her face was set in somber lines. When Mr. Merle's name was mentioned she shook her head, unbelieving of the cruelty of fate. She said it was very hard to believe.

"Sad," Weigand said. "Very sad indeed."

Miss Werty, he thought, was the best evidence he had yet seen to disprove any hints about the unsaintliness of Mr. Merle. Miss Werty marked the late Mr. Merle as ascetic. Miss Werty had been chosen for efficiency.

She proved it. Mr. Merle had arrived at 10:34 the previous morning. He had answered some mail—nothing of importance.

"A matter of a loan," she said. "And of a drive chairmanship. He was as efficient as he always was and as—as concise. He decided instantly as he always did—no or yes as the case might be."

He had left at 1:10 and had returned at ten minutes of three. He had dictated several letters and had gone, leaving them to be signed in the morning, at 4:35. Miss Werty, it was clear, was Mr. Merle's time clock. Weigand nodded and complimented her. He assured himself that none of the mail Miss Werty had opened for Mr. Merle had been of importance; that there had been two letters marked "personal" which she had not opened.

"By the way," he said, "can you tell me anything about Mr. Murdock? What time he came and went, for example?"

Miss Werty said, "Oh, I don't know, I'm sure," in a tone which indicated that Mr. Murdock had by no means been important enough to keep track of. Weigand pressed, gently. Had Mr. Murdock, for example, been in during the morning?

"Oh, yes," Miss Werty said. "Naturally. A little before Mr. Merle."

And he had remained—?

"I *really* can't say," Miss Werty said. "He was around during the morning I suppose. No doubt his secretary would know."

"No doubt," Weigand agreed. "Did he see Mr. Merle?"

"I believe Mr. Merle summoned him about noon," Miss Werty said. Her tone implied that the issuance of such a summons had been a regrettable, but minor, lapse on the part of Mr. Merle.

"And you were in the office at the time?" Weigand suggested. Miss Werty unexpectedly flushed.

"I summoned Mr. Murdock," she said, and was haughty. "Then I—I had some other duties, of course."

"Of course," Weigand agreed. "Was Murdock with Mr. Merle for any considerable time?"

"I'm sure I—" she began. "About an hour," she ended. "Mr. Merle sent Mr. Murdock somewhere and he left about ten minutes before Mr. Merle did." She looked at Bill Weigand with meaning, although it was not clear what the meaning was. "He was gone all afternoon," she said. "All afternoon. He didn't come back at all."

Weigand said it was all very interesting and thanked Miss Werty and praised the clarity and succinctness of her answers. Miss Werty left. The vice president smiled faintly, momentarily relaxed.

"The old girl didn't like Murdock," he said. "Call it professional jealousy. But don't think she didn't know every move he made."

"Every move?" Weigand repeated.

The vice president looked at the detective with calculation.

"I don't know," he said, "that any of us knew quite every move Mr. Murdock made. Except Mr. Merle, of course."

"Mr. Merle used him for—private errands?" Weigand suggested.

The vice president turned all vice president. He was sure he didn't know. His tone implied that the president of a bank could have no private errands to be done; that with such a man all was openly arrived at.

"I have a feeling that Murdock was Mr. Merle's—how would you say it—confidential man," Weigand said. "His—personal representative. You think not?"

"I'm sure I wouldn't know," the vice president said sternly. "I never supposed that Mr. Merle had—had need for a confidential man."

The vice president regarded the suggestion with distaste. He pushed it away with his fingertips.

"Right," Weigand said. "Now—we have reason to think that Mr. Merle drew a check for a considerable amount yesterday and that he gave it to someone. Or that someone took it. Would you have any way of telling us whether that is true?"

The vice president smiled and was patient. Mr. Merle's personal checkbook would, naturally, be the only source of such information. Weigand also was patient. He suggested that Mr. Merle might have several checkbooks for several purposes. He suggested that the bank records might show whether such a check had been cleared—whether any check drawn by Mr. Merle, for a probably considerable amount, had been cleared.

"Naturally," the vice president said, "Mr. Merle's account was frozen as soon as we heard of his death. No checks would be cleared."

Weigand agreed. That was the rule. It went into effect when the bank had definite notification of the death of a depositor.

"In fact, however," he pointed out, "checks do frequently go through after a person's death—checks drawn before death and reaching the bank afterward. But before official notification. Isn't that correct?"

The vice president supposed it happened.

Then, Weigand suggested, there might be just a chance that a check drawn by Mr. Merle, dropped into the mails the night before for deposit, say—or brought in just as the bank opened in the morning—might conceivably have been cashed? By someone who went through accustomed motions without analysis; possibly by someone who had not even heard of Mr. Merle's death, or not taken in the fact of his death as having any application to routine business at hand?

The vice president thought it possible. He would check. He sent out orders. He and Weigand sat and looked at each other.

"What did you think of Murdock, personally?" Weigand asked suddenly. The other man looked at him and raised eyebrows. Weigand did not amplify.

"I had very little contact with Mr. Murdock," the vice president said. "I knew very little of his relationship with Mr. Merle. I did not even know his exact duties."

Bill Weigand waited. The vice president reached into his mind and chose words carefully.

"I should not," he said, "I should not at all have taken him for a bank man. If I had met him elsewhere."

Weigand smiled slightly. The vice president did not smile. His expression did not, on the other hand, reject Bill Weigand's smile. Weigand lighted a cigarette, and an elderly man came in carrying an eyeshade in one hand and some papers in the other.

"Mr. Merle's statement," he said. "As of this morning. And Mr. Murdock's." He looked at the vice president and sighed. "I'm afraid there was a check," he said. He sighed again and went away. The vice president looked at the yellow records and at a check clipped to them. Without comment, he pushed the collection across the desk to Weigand.

The day before, George Merle had drawn a check for $10,000, made out to Oscar Murdock. The check, not endorsed, had come in, in the mail that morning. The bank had endorsed it by stamp and transferred the amount to Murdock's account, completing a transaction between dead men. Weigand raised eyebrows and looked at the vice president.

"Somebody slipped up," the vice president said. "As you suggested, Lieutenant. The rest, of course, was routine."

"Including the stamped endorsement," Weigand said, not as a question.

"Routine," the vice president agreed. "When we know both payee and payer. When it is entirely a deposit matter."

Weigand studied the check and the records for a moment longer. He shoved them back.

"Is it your check?" the vice president wanted to know. "The one you were interested in?"

Weigand thought it was. He thought that, later, they might want it, in which case a proper order would be forthcoming. Meanwhile—

"Does it clear anything up?" the vice president asked.

"No," Weigand said. "Not particularly."

Weigand turned it over in his mind as Mullins angled the Buick across town to the East River Drive, uptown to the Tri-Borough and along parkways and into quieter roads on Long Island. It didn't clear things up, particularly. It was not even certain that it was the check they were after. For why would that check be made out to Murdock, when it was meant for "L"? And why, if Murdock had it, would he take the chance of mailing it to the bank, knowing that it would inevitably suggest that he had been in at Merle's death?

"Maybe," Mullins said, "Merle was just paying off a bet. Maybe it hasn't anything to do with us, one way or the other."

"Right," Weigand said. He considered. "But I think it has," he said.

He had a sudden idea, which fitted nearly enough. "Suppose—" he began. Then he saw a small sign pointing up a graveled road. It said: STATE POLICE BARRACKS.

"There," he said, pointing. Mullins swung the car up the road and in the graveled circle before the barracks.

Weigand went in and came out with a tall, vigorous man in civilian clothes.

"Captain Sullivan," he told Mullins. "Captain, Sergeant Mullins."

With the man from the Criminal Identification Department of the State Police guiding them, they looped back to the road. The town of Elmcroft began around the next bend. It ended around the bend which followed. Two miles beyond it, they swung off on a private road between stone pillars. They left behind a band of evergreens screening the house from the road.

It was a large house, lying white under the June sun. It lay among lawns, and off to the left a man was riding a power-mower in narrowing circles, the lawn newly neat wherever he had been. When they stopped the car the smell of newly cut grass was fresh and Bill Weigand's mind was ruffled by memories which the fragrance evoked.

"It's odd," he said, unexpectedly to himself, "how odors make you remember things. More than music. Or isn't that true of you, Captain?"

The captain said he had never thought of it particularly. Mullins said that with him it was tunes.

"And," he said, "every so often when I'm shaving I think of collecting for magazine subscriptions when I was a kid. I think of a Hundredth Street and between Second and Third Avenues."

"Why?" Weigand asked.

"Hell," Mullins said, "how should I know, Loot?"

They got out and stood looking at the house.

"It's a fine place," Captain Sullivan said. "One of the best around here. Over beyond the house they can go right down to the sound and a private beach. Pretty nice."

If they didn't want to go to the private beach, there was always the private swimming pool. At the side of the house toward the east, where the sun would reach it in the morning and shade cover it in the afternoon, was a broad stretch of level lawn. Beyond it, perhaps two hundred feet from the house, was a pool, and to the north of the pool a low structure, clapboarded and white like the house, evidently contained dressing rooms. Between the bathhouse and the pool, and along the side of the pool nearest the house, were deck chairs and tables, some of them protected by colored umbrellas. And as they watched, a girl in a white bathing suit came out of the bathhouse, walked out on a diving board, bounced once and arched into the water.

"Miss Merle," he said. "Miss Ann Merle. The daughter." His tone sounded slightly disapproving. "You'd think she—" he started to amplify. "Only she wouldn't. Not Ann Merle."

"What?" Weigand wanted to know. "Wear a black bathing suit?"

Captain Sullivan laughed briefly. He admitted that there was, after all, no reason why a daughter recently bereaved should, as a gesture of mourning, eschew a swim in a private swimming pool.

"Only," he said, "it still don't look right."

The girl swam the length of the pool, swam halfway back again and turned suddenly toward the side nearest them. She pulled herself up and looked at them. Then she came out, twisting herself expertly over the edge. She said, "Hi!"

"Hi, Ann," Captain Sullivan called across the lawn. Weigand looked at him quickly. It was unexpected.

"'Lo, Teddy," Ann Merle said and moved a little way toward them. They walked across the grass toward her and she stopped and stood waiting. She was a very pretty girl from a distance and she was an even prettier girl as they approached. As they came closer, she pulled off a white bathing cap and her hair was black and smooth. She had deep blue eyes in a tanned face and all that the bathing suit did not hide of her was smoothly tanned. She stood easily, waiting for them, her arms hanging naturally by her sides and her hands, a little cupped, easy in repose. She was clearly undisturbed at the approach of the law; at the approach of three men, she was superbly confident.

"What," she said, when they were near enough so that she did not need to raise her voice, "brings you—oh, Father, of course."

"Ann," Captain Sullivan said, "these men are from New York.

Homicide men. They're investigating the—your father's death."

He introduced them, and the girl was quiet and serious.

"I supposed somebody would come," she said. "To—to look us over. I hope you don't think all this"—she waved at the pool and included herself in the term—"means any of us is taking Father's death casually."

"No," Bill Weigand said. "I was just telling the captain here—." He broke off. Ann Merle smiled at Captain Sullivan.

"Teddy doesn't approve?" she said. "No, I suppose he doesn't. Teddy has trouble with us, don't you, Teddy."

Captain Sullivan smiled, with no great enjoyment.

"She and her brother drive like hell, Lieutenant," he said. "The boys are all the time picking them up for it. That's what she means." He spoke to the girl. "You'll do what seems all right to you, Ann," he said. "It's not my business."

"Anyway," Ann said, "it isn't what the lieutenant wants to know about. Unless he thinks I'm—callous. And hence a suspicious character. And I don't think he does."

She looked at Bill Weigand.

"I'm not callous, Lieutenant," she said. "I'm not forgetting about Father."

Her voice was sober.

"I want to help," she said. "We all do."

Bill Weigand was sure she did. He agreed when she said that they would want to go up to the house. He agreed further when she said that she would get her brother to talk to him. He assured her that the whole matter was routine; that he would like permission to go over her father's desk; that, as a matter still of routine, he wanted to meet the family. Herself, her brother—. He paused.

"Aunt Mae," she filled in. "That's all the family there is, really. Jamie's around, of course, but he's—he's just a—a guest. And then there's Arnold Wickersham Potts, of course. Wicky."

"Is there?" Weigand said. "Does Mr. Potts live here?"

"Oh, no," Ann Merle said. "Not here. Not at the house. He rents the guest house. Down by the beach. But of course you've heard of Mr.

Potts. A. Wickersham Potts? He doesn't use the Arnold much."

"No," Weigand said. "I never heard of Mr. Potts."

"No?" the girl said. "The organist? He's really celebrated, you know. Among organists. He plays at St. Andrew's on Park. Where we go—where we've always gone in winters. When we're in town."

"Does he?" Bill Weigand said. "I don't know many organists."

He did not suppose that he would intimately know Mr. Potts—a tall, dark man, he supposed, with rather lank hair and a long, sharp, delicate face. His tone dismissed Mr. Potts. He ran over in his mind the things that might matter—the things and people. Ann Merle and her brother Joshua, Jameson possibly, the aunt possibly, George Merle's checkbook, details of the will from the lawyer in Elmcroft, possibly a servant or two to corroborate details of George Merle's movements the day before. And then? Then back to town, probably, with background in his mind—with Merle fitted into a habitat so that he could be seen against it, with whatever oblique light on Merle's character, the place he lived, the books on his library shelves, the pictures on the walls, might shed. And then, in town, back to slow digging—digging into Murdock's past and Laurel Burke's, digging into the real character and the unadvertised activities of the respected gentleman who had come to so awkward an end in the little Madison Avenue flat. It was going to take long digging, Weigand decided; longer than the inspector would approve. Unless unexpected things happened—things of which there was now no sign.

An hour and a half later his views as to the probable future of the case were unchanged. He sat at Mr. Merle's desk and reviewed from his notes.

The checkbook had given him something. It was not certain what that something meant—what a check, made out not the day before but the day before that, for $10,000 and entered on the stub, not to Murdock but to cash, had to do with three bullets in Mr. Merle's chest. You could suppose it was the same check, entered as cash in the checkbook and made out on its face to Murdock. That was an interesting supposition, because it meant that Merle had not wanted the record of the payment to show to anyone who might be tempted to look at the checkbook entries. A housemaid dusting the room in his absence, perhaps?

An inquisitive member of the family? Because the book was in an unlocked drawer of the desk.

He had found that the servants, and particularly the chauffeur who had driven George Merle to the train, agreed with Joshua Merle as to the time of the elder Merle's departure for the city the day before. They also agreed with Joshua Merle's account of his own movements. Merle himself was calmer than the night before and easier. And he had nothing to add. He had spent the day idly in town; he had dropped in at Charles for dinner and there someone, ostensibly a policeman, had telephoned him of his father's death. He had met Jameson outside, told Jameson the news and asked Jameson to go around to the precinct house with him.

"By the way," Weigand said, "this accident in training. You and Mr. Jameson were together at the time? I mean, you were both hurt in the same accident?"

Joshua Merle's face showed unpleasant memories. He nodded.

"In the same plane," he said. "A two-motored trainer with dual controls. Jamie and I were taking turns handling her. The next step, if we'd come through that all right, would have been the real thing."

Weigand made a sound of sympathy.

"What happened?" he said.

"I cracked her up," he said. "Coming in. I miscalculated and—cracked her up. And Jamie and I didn't walk away. Neither of us walked anywhere so well afterward. His right knee got cracked to hell and I've only got part of a right foot. Not enough for the Navy."

"You were piloting at the time?" Weigand said.

The dark young man nodded bitterly.

"It was my pigeon," he said. "And did I foul it up." He looked at Weigand darkly. "Snafu to a fare-you-well," he said. "Not only myself but poor Jamie too."

Weldon Jameson had not seemed nearly so bitter about it. It had been, he said, something that might happen to anyone. A lot of guys cracked up in training. They were lucky, in a way, to have got out as well as they had. There was nothing to indicate that he held any bitterness toward Joshua Merle. On the contrary.

"Poor Josh can't forget it," he said. "He keeps blaming himself—seems to feel that he owes me something. I keep telling him it's just the fortunes of—well, of war. If I'd been flying her, likely as not I'd have cracked up too. There was quite a wind and probably we got a downdraft or something. He's a sweet guy, old Josh."

He paused at that point and looked at Weigand.

"As a matter of fact," he said, "that's really why I'm more or less living here. Josh feels that he's got to—well, repay me, I guess, for what happened. And I haven't got any money and he has—so." He shook his head. Weigand waited and let his waiting seem expectant.

"Hell," Jameson said, "I'd actually rather be on my own. That is—I've got to start some time. But I hate to tell Josh that, because—well, he's a funny sort of bloke. Sensitive. As long as he can feel that he's doing something for me it maybe helps him get over it. You see what I mean?"

"Yes," Weigand told him.

"Of course," Jameson said, and he smiled suddenly, "I don't pretend that this isn't a very comfortable spot. It's a break for me, all right."

"Naturally," Bill Weigand said. "Of course that enters into it."

Jameson said he was damned right it did.

He had stood up and started to limp away, looking a very attractive young man.

"By the way," Weigand said, "Mr. Merle was lucky he ran into you just after he heard about his father. It was a good time to have a friend along."

"Yes, I suppose so," Jameson said. "I don't know that I helped much. But probably it was a lucky break for Josh—running into anybody just then would have been."

He stood a moment and his face was graver.

"It's bad for Josh," he said. "He was fond of the old man. I'm glad I happened to be around when he needed somebody."

He went on, after that.

Ann Merle had changed into a dark blue sports dress when she talked to Weigand the second time, but her long brown legs were still bare. She corroborated the time of her father's departure for the city, and also the times her brother and Jameson had left. She herself had been around until midafternoon and then had driven to a tennis club near by. Later, after a couple of sets, she and a friend—sex and identity left vague—had driven into New York for cocktails and dinner. It was late when they drove back.

"By the way," Weigand said, "did you know that your brother was going to be at Charles for dinner?"

The girl shook her head and said, "No."

"Why?" she said.

"Somebody did," Weigand told her. "I'm curious to know who. You didn't know. Mr. Jameson ran into him there entirely by accident, I gather. The police didn't know, although they were supposed to have telephoned him there. And somebody did telephone him there."

"I didn't know," she said. "I should think obviously it was Mr. Murdock. The man who killed Father."

"Probably," Weigand agreed. "Unfortunately I can't ask him."

"Which," the girl said, "brings up a point. If Mr. Murdock killed Father and then himself, why isn't the case closed? Why are you here at all?"

"Odds and ends," Bill told her, evenly. "We try to leave things tidy. And, of course, Murdock didn't leave any confession. It's merely an assumption that he killed your father. A reasonable assumption, of course—probably a valid assumption. But we still like to have a last look around."

"A last look around," the girl repeated. "You are very thorough, Lieutenant Weigand."

Bill Weigand said they always tried to be thorough. He asked her if he might see her aunt for a moment. He saw Aunt Mae for a moment— Aunt Mae dressed in black, with evidence of past tears, very dignified and grave and, in a grave and dignified manner, very vindictive toward Oscar Murdock. She was inclined to think that the laxity of the police in allowing him to escape punishment was difficult to excuse. Weigand forebore to point out that the police could hardly have done more to Murdock than was already done; he thanked Mrs. Mae Burnwood,

widowed sister of the late George Merle, and let her go. He found
Mullins, who had finished with the servants and added nothing to what
they knew, sitting at the pool in comfort; he found Captain Sullivan,
talking with Ann Merle. He indicated that he had finished.

"But of course," Ann said, "you're staying to lunch. You and Teddy
and—Mr. Mullins."

Bill Weigand started to refuse and Captain Sullivan looked at him
with fixed hope in his eyes. After all, Weigand decided, they had to eat
somewhere. He thanked Ann Merle and accepted. Captain Sullivan
looked pleased and grateful.

· 10 ·

WEDNESDAY, 1:15 P.M. TO 4:10 P.M.

The sun was warm and bright on the lawn stretching from house to swimming pool, but the shadow began to creep out from the house toward the pool. At first it was only an edge of shadow, reaching no farther than the serving table set between the French doors which led into the long, cool living room. They sat in the sun, not at one table but as they chose, at several small tables. And they did not hurry; almost at once Bill Weigand decided that he had made a mistake in staying. Because this was going on—nobody could guess how long it was going on.

First the table against the house was a bar—first and last it was a bar. The Negro butler in a white coat—the butler named Meggs—brought out trays of bottles and glasses and two maids assisted with ice and cocktail shakers.

"Sit here," Ann Merle suggested; and Bill Weigand sat with her at a little table for four on the flagstoned terrace. Captain Sullivan of the State Police sat in a third chair rather eagerly, and Mullins looked doubtful. "Here you are, Sergeant," Weldon Jameson told him, and Mullins sat at another table a little way off with Jameson and Joshua Merle. But almost at once Jameson got up and moved across to take the fourth chair at the table where Weigand and Sullivan sat with Ann

111

Merle. Then Mrs. Burnwood came out through one of the French doors, a little to Weigand's surprise, and the men stood up briefly. She sat with her nephew and Mullins. Meggs began to shake daiquiris expertly, and a round, pink man in slacks and a pale blue shirt came around the house from the direction of the beach. He blinked a little in the sun, pleasantly.

"Hi," Ann Merle called. "Just in time. Sit down somewhere. Oh—come here first."

The round little man came gently across the flagstones, smiling at everybody. He came to stand near Ann. He said, "Good morning, my dear," in a gentle voice and "Hello, Theodore" to Sullivan. He looked at Bill Weigand with an air of pleased expectancy.

"Pottsy," Ann said, "this is Lieutenant Weigand. Lieutenant, this is Mr. Potts—Wickersham Potts. The organist."

Weigand blinked and took the hand Mr. Potts held out. It was a firm hand, solid and confident.

"Good morning, Lieutenant," Mr. Potts said, as if he really believed it was a good morning, and was pleased for his own sake and the lieutenant's sake. "I'm very glad, sir." He meant that he was glad to meet Weigand, evidently; he sounded as if he were glad.

"How do you do?" Bill said. In spite of himself, his voice had a note of surprise. The note, Bill Weigand was instantly conscious, did not escape Mr. Potts. Mr. Potts did not look like a man from whom much would escape in inflection, in nuance. But Mr. Potts made nothing of it. If Weigand had expected a different sort of Mr. Potts, and was surprised by what he got, that was interesting but unabashing to Mr. Potts. He smiled at Weigand as if already he liked him.

"On leave, Lieutenant?" he inquired gently, his eyes just noticing Weigand's gray suit.

"Oh," Ann said. "Not an army lieutenant. A police lieutenant." She sobered. "About Father, you know, Pottsy."

"Of course," Mr. Potts said. "Naturally. It was a very tragic thing—a very cruel and tragic thing. It is strange what people will do to one another."

"Yes," Weigand said.

"The human mind," Mr. Potts said. "A strange and alarming thing, don't you think so, Lieutenant? Do sit down."

Bill Weigand sat down and Sullivan sat down.

"Good morning, Mr. Potts," Weldon Jameson said, and there was a note in his voice which seemed to challenge the organist. Mr. Potts turned a little and regarded Jameson.

"Oh," he said. "Good morning, Mr. Jameson."

He turned back to Ann, with no impoliteness but as if he and Jameson had finished a long and interesting conversation and it was time to turn his attention elsewhere.

"In the cottage," he said, "there are two cans of beans, a can of noodle soup, and some bread which I fear is rather stale. So, if I may?"

"Pottsy!" Ann said. "You know we were expecting you."

"You are very kind, my dear," Mr. Potts said. "You are all very kind. I hoped you were. Ah—your aunt."

He nodded and smiled to Bill Weigand, indicating by both his renewed pleasure in their meeting, and went across to Mrs. Burnwood. After a moment, he sat with her and her nephew and Mullins.

"He's a dear," Ann told Bill Weigand. She did not care whether Mr. Potts heard or not, and the tables were close enough so that conversations tangled in the quiet air.

Mr. Potts turned from his conversation with Sergeant Mullins and raised his eyebrows at her and smiled. He turned back to Mullins.

"Yours must be an interesting profession, Sergeant," he said. "But sad—essentially sad."

"Yeah," Mullins said. "I know what you mean."

"Does he?" Ann said to Bill Weigand.

"Yes," Bill told her. "Probably."

The butler in the white coat offered a tray. Pale martinis were on it, with the barely perceptible dullness of the oil from lemon peel on their surfaces. There were no olives. It was an opportunity not to be missed, and Bill did not miss it. There were daiquiris with no frosting of sugar on the rims of the glasses. Ann said, faithfully, Captain Sullivan took daiquiris.

"Scotch, sir?" Meggs suggested to Weldon Jameson. He turned the tray and Jameson lifted scotch from it. Meggs turned away and a dark girl in a green uniform offered canapés. It had somehow the earmarks of a cocktail party—a cocktail party at one thirty in the afternoon. But apparently it was only luncheon at the Merles'. Jameson's first contact with his scotch brought the level halfway down the glass. Bill Weigand drank his martini slowly at first. Meggs was an artist. He drank more rapidly. His glass and that of Ann Merle went down together, both empty. Captain Sullivan was slower. Meggs gravitated back and removed the glasses and Weigand watched him go with regret. Meggs returned with fresh glasses. Weigand, sipping, discovered that the new drink was freshly made. Meggs was quite a man.

But he should not be sitting here in the sun, a lotus drinker. He should be in Elmcroft, seeing a lawyer, he should be in New York, finding a murderer.

"You have a very delightful place here, Miss Merle," he said. "A very beautiful place."

It was nice, Ann Merle agreed.

"We all like it," she said. "Don't we, Jamie?"

"Very much," Jameson said. "Very much, darling."

It was a casual "darling."

A car stopped somewhere and a car door slammed. A tall young man in tennis whites came around the house and looked at them.

"Stan!" Ann Merle called. "Hello, Stan."

The tall young man came across to the table. His face was grave.

"Ann," he said. "It's a hell of a thing."

"Yes, Stan," Ann Merle said. "It's a hell of a thing."

"Are you all right?" the man said. "I wanted to see if you were all right." He looked at her face intently.

"Don't I look all right?" she said. "Yes, I'm all right, Stan. You were sweet to—you don't know all these people, do you, Stan. This is Lieutenant Weigand. A police lieutenant."

"Oh," the young man said. "Hello, Lieutenant."

"Stanley Goode," Ann said.

Bill Weigand shook hands with Stanley Goode, who was a good enough tennis player to be a tennis bum, and had too much money to be a bum of any kind. And who was one of the few in the first ten not in a uniform of some sort.

"Hello, Captain," Stanley Goode said to Sullivan. "Jamie."

"Hello," Sullivan said, with no perceptible enthusiasm. "Ann's all right."

"Sure," Goode said. "Everybody's all right. What's murder among friends?"

"Stan!" Ann said. "For God's sake, Stan!"

"Sorry," Goode said. "Everybody looks so damn comfortable. Don't they, Jamie?"

"Why not?" Jameson said.

"Sit down, Stan," Ann said. "Have a drink. Don't be a fool."

"Stan is young," Mr. Potts said from the next table. "Very young. He believes in forms. How are you, Stan?"

"Fine," Stanley Goode said. "Fine as silk."

He sat down on the grass by Ann's chair. When Meggs came around again he took a scotch. Ann bent and said something to him.

"I know," he said. "I'm sorry. It's the whole damn thing—all the damned things."

"Not again?" she said.

"Why not?" he said. "Why the hell not? They've said it; they stick to it."

Ann said she was sorry.

"It doesn't matter," Stanley Goode said. "You've got enough to— I'm sorry as hell about your dad, Ann."

"I know," Ann said. "You're sweet."

The maids began to pass plates and, after the plates, great trays of salad, cold meat, jellied consommes. It was time for food, Bill Weigand thought—after three martinis it was time for food. He ate, listening to conversation around him. Ann pushed her food back and forth on her plate and lifted her eyebrows to Meggs.

"Bring me a rum collins, Meggs," she said when he came over. He brought the rum collins, the glass frosted.

Jameson drank thirstily and ate a little. Sullivan drank not at all and ate a good deal. Stanley Goode refused food, saying he had already eaten. He sipped his drink slowly but persistently.

At the other table, Mrs. Burnwood and Mr. A. Wickersham Potts were drinking sherry out of small glasses, and Mullins, already reddening slightly, was drinking old-fashioneds. By the color, Joshua Merle was drinking a cuba libre. But nobody was showing anything, if you discounted the reddening of Mullins, which Weigand was willing to do.

Or were they showing something? Later in the afternoon, Bill Weigand wondered if they had not been. He wondered if even then, before the fireworks started, there had not been a tension in the group on the terrace, with the shadow from the house gradually reaching out over them, synchronizing its coolness with the sun's increasing warmth as if the Merles had planned it so. As, of course, in a sense they had when they built the big white house and put a flagged terrace on the side which would be shady in the afternoon, and left the pool beyond the farthest reach of shade, so that it would be warm there as long as the sun held.

If there was tension, Bill Weigand was only half conscious of it at the time. Relaxed by the cocktails, even his never too disturbing sense of urgency had left him—there on the terrace, with the city a long way off, he tentatively accepted the present as a pause in the day's occupation. "Which," he quoted to himself, "is known as the children's hour." They had finished their food and were drinking iced coffee—he, at any rate, was drinking iced coffee—when he returned to full awareness and began, casually at first and then more acutely, to wonder whether there was not something in the air among these pleasant people which needed his attention—which was, after all, somehow a part of his occupation.

After the tables had been cleared and only glasses remained—and only one or two of them, he gathered, containing anything so mild as his iced coffee and Mr. Potts's evident iced tea—people began to move around. Jameson got up, carrying his glass, and wandered away somewhere. And when he wandered back he limped over to the table at which Joshua Merle sat and stood there, looking down at Merle and Merle's aunt and the round, gentle organist. Stan Goode got up and pulled Ann by the hand from her chair and they went out into the sun and sat side by side in deck chairs. Captain Sullivan looked after them, but did not move.

After a little, Mr. Potts got up from the table and, although there seemed to be no purpose in his movements, they brought him to the table at which Bill Weigand sat, thinking it was time to break loose from this languid comfort and be about his business. Potts sat down.

"Conscience," he said with no preliminaries, "is a strange thing, don't you think, Lieutenant?"

"How strange?" Weigand asked him.

"I was thinking of conscience as a compulsion," Potts said. "A compulsion to repay—to discharge an obligation. An obligation we may so easily overestimate."

"Not," Bill Weigand said, "the conscience of a murderer. That isn't what you're thinking of."

"Not entirely," Mr. Potts said. "That would be interesting too, I should suppose. How must a man feel when he has taken human life?" He paused, reflectively. "Personally," he said, "I have never committed a murder."

He said it simply, as one might confer information—as one might say that, personally, he never drank beer. He did not at all say it as anything which was obvious on the face of things; he spoke as if Bill Weigand might have been wondering.

"No," Weigand said, not quite smiling. "A great many people haven't, Mr. Potts. A surprising number of people haven't."

"Well," Mr. Potts said, "a surprising number of people have. It depends on what surprises you."

"Yes," Bill Weigand said. "What surprises you, Mr. Potts?"

"Very little," Mr. Potts said. "Very little indeed, Lieutenant. I am sometimes surprised at how many things do not surprise me." He considered this. "I presume," he said, "that there is a deficiency somewhere which would account for that. But it could hardly be a vitamin deficiency, would you think, Lieutenant? Because I get a very adequate supply of vitamins, I'm sure."

"It could," Bill Weigand told him, "be a deficiency in illusions."

Mr. Potts looked at Bill and thought it over and nodded.

"That is very true, Lieutenant," he said. "I am not surprised to find that you have hit on that. It could very well be a deficiency in illusions." He paused again. "And, of course, I find people very interesting," he said. "I take a quite real interest in people. But I do not suppose that surprises you, Lieutenant?"

"No," Bill said. "I can't say that surprises me."

Mr. Potts stood up.

"People are very interesting," he repeated. "Often even small things about them are very revealing. At the moment, I am particularly interested in conscience—not necessarily the conscience of a murderer, because I have seen nothing which reveals that. Not here, at any rate."

Weigand stood up.

"Do you want to tell me something, Mr. Potts?" he said.

A. Wickersham Potts did not seem surprised at that, either. He smiled faintly and did not answer directly.

"I merely wondered whether you shared my interest in the effect of conscience on an individual," he said. "Conscience which amounts to a sense of obligation—probably to an excessive sense of obligation."

He looked across at Ann and Stanley Goode.

"Ann is a very sweet child, Lieutenant," he said. "She is much more broken up over her father's death than you might think. She is not at all callous."

"I hadn't thought she was," Weigand assured him.

"No," Mr. Potts said. "I didn't think you thought that, Lieutenant. She is under something of a strain at the moment, in addition to that, of course. She is—how shall I say it—being offered an obligation. A share of an obligation. She has other plans, but she is a very sensitive child in many ways."

He paused again and continued to regard Ann Merle and Goode.

"It's too bad about Goode," he said. "Very bad heart, you know. At least, the doctors say so. I must say he doesn't look it. I—"

He left whatever he had planned to add to dissipate and went off, not as if he had any particular destination. He went, generally, toward the house. And what, Bill wondered, was that about?

He stood up with his glass, intending to thank Ann and be about his business. But he decided that, instead—and since Ann and Stanley Goode were evidently engrossed—he might talk to Mrs. Burnwood. He crossed to the table where she still sat.

"—and it's time somebody told you straight out, Joshua," she was saying. "Your whole attitude is—is unwholesome. That's the only word for it."

"You don't understand, Aunt Mae," Josh Merle said. His face was darkly intent. "You simply don't understand Jamie—oh, hello, Weigand."

Weigand's eyes sought Mullins, but Mullins had disappeared.

"It was very good of you—" he began. But Mrs. Burnwood was not listening. She was looking beyond him, and young Merle half turned in his chair and looked in the same direction. Suddenly Merle swore, and his voice was angry.

Bill Weigand turned and, no doubt because he was not so deficient in illusions as Mr. Potts, he was surprised. Laurel Burke was coming across the lawn from the car circle. Behind her a car turned on the circle, spitting gravel, and went down toward the county road. Miss Burke apparently had come by taxi and did not plan an immediate return.

Weigand did not watch her. He turned quickly and watched the faces of those who were watching her. Mrs. Burnwood's face showed surprise and uncertainty. It did not, Weigand thought, show recognition. But Josh Merle knew Laurel Burke and did not want her there. Weigand looked for Mr. Potts to see whether this surprised him, but Mr. Potts was not present to be unsurprised. Nor, for that matter, was Weldon Jameson. Then Weldon Jameson came out from the living room through one of the French doors. He had not seen Laurel Burke yet. When, seeing so many eyes on a single point, he turned and did see Laurel Burke, his back was to Weigand and there was nothing to go on but the set of shoulders and the movement of body. These, Weigand discovered, were nothing at all to go on.

Ann and Stanley Goode had their backs to the house and were still engrossed. They did not turn until Laurel Burke spoke.

Miss Burke was entirely conscious of the entrance she was making.

That was evident in each considered step she took, each movement of her body. Her body had many movements. She wore a print dress which let the movements of her body be seen; she had white artificial flowers in her hair to serve as hat. Even from fifty feet her bright fingernails caught the sun and sparkled redly.

"Hello, everybody," Laurel Burke said in her lowest and most controlled tones—the tones which were almost good enough. "Hello, everybody. I'm Laurel Burke."

Nobody said anything. Miss Burke did not seem to expect that anybody would say anything. She came toward them, smiling pleasantly, ignoring what she might have interpreted as a lack of welcoming enthusiasm.

It was not clear whether she recognized any of the people looking at her. She did not directly, specially, look at anyone. Possibly her glance lingered a moment as it passed Weldon Jameson, but that was guesswork. Perhaps it lingered again as it encountered the dark, now definitely angry, face of Joshua Merle. But neither Merle nor Jameson said anything in reply to her greeting, and she seemed not at all surprised that they did not.

"I thought," Laurel Burke said when she was close enough to speak without raising her carefully controlled voice, "I thought I'd better come and introduce myself. I'm Laurel Burke."

Ann Merle was coming across the lawn toward them now, with Stanley Goode behind her. She did not say anything.

"Don't," Miss Burke said, "tell me I'm not welcome. Really I feel as if I were coming home. I've heard so *much* about this beautiful place."

"How do you do, Miss Burke," Ann Merle said. Her young voice was level, without expression. "I'm afraid I don't—"

"You," Laurel Burke said, "must be Ann."

"I'm Ann Merle," Ann told her. "This is the Merle place."

"Of course, dear," Laurel said. "The taxi man knew instantly. I had him go on, of course. I knew I would be here—some time."

Joshua Merle limped forward suddenly until he was quite close to her.

"I don't know what you want," he said. "You—"

"Don't you, Mr. Merle?" Laurel said. "It *is* Mr. Merle, isn't it?"

"You know damn well," Merle told her.

"And, as you put it, you know damn well what I want," Laurel said, but she still kept her voice down. "What—*we* want." Her accent was heavy on the "we."

"Who," Mrs. Burnwood said, with a good deal of distaste "is this— this Miss Burke, Joshua?"

Laurel Burke did not give Joshua time to answer.

"Mrs. Burnwood?" she said. "Of course. Why, my dear, your brother's girl friend, of course. His very *dear* girl friend."

There was no mistaking what she meant. She had not intended there should be. There was a complete hush over the terrace. It was so complete that the sound of ice falling into a glass from Meggs's silver tongs was like a crash.

"Oh," Laurel said, and her voice was sweet—was very sweet. "I don't believe you *knew.* I really don't believe Georgey told you. He was *so* secretive, wasn't he. Poor, dear Georgey."

"You—!" Joshua Merle said, and moved very close to her. She did not draw back, but her voice was harder when she spoke.

"I wouldn't, Josh Merle," she said. "I sure as hell wouldn't. You might hurt your little brother." She paused. "Or, of course, your little sister," she said. "Your father's youngest child, whatever the brat turns out to be."

Everybody looked at her with a different look.

"Oh," Laurel said, "you can't see anything yet. But you will, my dears." She looked at them, and now there was no longer an attempt at suavity. "You sure as hell will. About December, the doctor says."

Mrs. Burnwood detached herself from a world which contained Laurel Burke and spoke across the unlimited space she had opened between them.

"I do not believe you," she said, giving each word its own distinct finality.

"No?" Laurel Burke said. "Well, my lawyer does."

And if Mrs. Burnwood's tone was distant, Miss Burke's tone was assured—utterly assured. If Miss Burke was lying, she lied like an expert.

"Lieutenant Weigand," Mrs. Burnwood said, across almost as great a distance, "do we have to accept this, Captain Sullivan?"

"No," Sullivan said. "You can order her off your grounds. She's trespassing."

"Yes, Mrs. Burnwood," Bill Weigand said. "You can do that. If you want to."

"Oh, Lieutenant," Laurel Burke said, "how nice to see you again."

"Is it?" Bill Weigand asked her.

"Lieutenant," Ann Merle said. "Do you know Miss Burke?"

Weigand nodded slowly. He said he had talked to her.

"About your father's murder, Miss Merle," he said. He let it lie there.

"Then," Ann said, "she did know father. She was—what she says she was?"

"She knew your father, Miss Merle," Weigand said. "She may have been." He paused a moment. "I'd talk to her, if I were you—all of you. Although, as Sullivan says, you can throw her out."

"I think the lieutenant is so intelligent, don't you?" Miss Burke said, to nobody in particular. "And those drinks you all have do look so refreshing on such a warm afternoon."

Mrs. Burnwood turned and walked, without hurrying, with the stiffest of possible backs, across the terrace and through one of the French doors. Only after she had gone did anyone speak. Then it was Ann Merle.

"Meggs," she said, "Miss Burke would like a drink."

"Rye," Miss Burke said. "And soda if you've got it."

"Yes'm," Meggs said. He said it reproachfully. The very notion, his voice said, that the Merle establishment would be at any time, under any conceivable circumstances, without soda! Meggs, Bill Weigand decided afterward, was the only person who really got under Laurel Burke's skin throughout that long afternoon and evening, during which so many people tried to. Meggs convicted her of ignorance and of gaucherie with what, in his mouth, was a single syllable.

With a drink, Laurel Burke became a guest. It was interesting to watch the change. With a drink, she got a chair. With a chair, she became part of the group on the terrace, entitled to all privileges appertaining. Men stood until she was seated, Meggs moved a small table within reach of her hand, Meggs opened a box of cigarettes and put it by her drink. When she took a cigarette, Josh Merle, although his face was still dark and angry, bent toward her with a light.

"Thank you," Miss Burke said, politely. She considered. "You are all very kind," she told them.

Mr. Potts was back from wherever he had been, Bill Weigand noticed. He looked at Miss Burke with interest but without surprise.

"Weigand," Joshua Merle said.

"Yes?" Bill Weigand said.

"You say this—this Miss Burke could have been what she says she was?"

"She could have been," Weigand said. "I don't know that she was."

"You think she was?" Merle wanted to know.

"I think she could have been," Weigand said. "Naturally, I don't know that she is going to have your father's child, Mr. Merle. I don't know that she's going to have anybody's child."

"Ask my doctor," Laurel Burke said, shortly.

"I imagine they will, Miss Burke," Bill Weigand said. "I imagine they'll do just that. I suppose you are thinking about a paternity suit? Against the estate?"

"If they want it that way," Laurel Burke said. "I don't insist on it. I don't mind it."

"In spite of the fact," Bill reminded her, "that you lived in the Madison Avenue place as Murdock's wife?"

She could, Laurel Burke said, get around that all right.

"Plenty of people knew that was a gag," she said. "*Plenty* of people."

There was, Bill Weigand thought, a definite meaning in her emphasis on plenty. She might mean that some of them were in the group which heard her. It sounded as if she did mean that.

Bill Weigand looked at the group—Jameson, Merle, Ann Merle, Potts, Sullivan and himself and Mullins—who had also come back from wherever he had been—and Stanley Goode. And, of course, Meggs, circulating again with drinks. Everybody took drinks; almost abstractedly, Bill Weigand took one himself.

He waited for Ann or Josh Merle to deny—perhaps to deny heatedly—that their father was capable of living the kind of life Laurel Burke was saying he had lived; the kind of life which implied a surreptitious relationship with a girl such as Laurel, carried on under the cover of his secretary's name; all of which implied, in essence, a series of mean assignations in a hide-out—a life lacking entirely in the dignity George Merle had otherwise seemed to prize. But neither Ann nor Joshua challenged the girl on those grounds. These, he concluded, were wise children.

"What is going to be your story, Miss Burke?" Josh Merle asked. "Why should we pay off? I gather you want us to pay you off?"

"I want you to support your father's youngest child, Mr. Merle," she said. "I hoped you would want to."

Merle told her to come off it. He said she wanted them to support her. Because of her nuisance value. She opened her eyes wide in apparent astonishment and said that she thought he was taking a very unkind attitude. She said he wasn't at all like his father.

"Your father was always terribly sweet to me," she said.

Merle said, "Hell!" with emphasis and looked at Weigand.

"He used to take me to the most interesting places," she said, as if Merle had not spoken. "To night clubs like—like the Zero Club."

Again there was an odd emphasis. It was on the name of the club, which Bill Weigand knew, it being a part of his business to know them all. The Zero Club was in a basement and it was so dimly lighted that the face of a companion floated dimly across a table. It was a place where the chances of running into people—save in the purely physical sense, which was always probable—were reassuringly slight. If you wanted to be reassured, as George Merle must have. But there seemed no clear reason why Laurel Burke had gone to the trouble of mentioning it.

"Do any of you know the Zero Club?" she asked, "such an *interesting place.*"

She looked around. Weigand could not see that her glance lingered on any of them.

"Yes," Mr. Potts said, unexpectedly. "A very odd place indeed, Miss Burke. Why?"

"Oh," she said, "I just wondered. You'd like it, I'm sure—all of you. Mr. Jameson—you'd like it. Mr. Merle."

The two men looked at her. Joshua Merle said he doubted it.

"As a matter of fact," Jameson said, "I don't like it particularly. Any part of it."

"Really, Mr. Jameson?" she said. "Really? Do you like it, Miss Merle?"

"I like to see the people I'm with," Ann said. "I'm not afraid of people's seeing me."

"Why, of course not, Miss Merle," Laurel Burke said. "Why should you be?"

"What is your story?" Joshua Merle insisted. "If you've got a story."

"Why," Laurel said, "just what you suppose, Mr. Merle. Your father met me and was attracted and—things just happened. He rented me that dear little apartment and—"

"Under Murdock's name," Bill Weigand said. "So you could pose as Murdock's wife?"

"Your dear father was so careful, Mr. Merle," Laurel Burke said. "Of course he was such an important man."

"Did Murdock—find you for Mr. Merle?" Weigand asked.

She looked at him.

"I think that's a terrible thing to say, Lieutenant," she said. "So exactly what a policeman would think."

"It's what I think," Joshua Merle told her. "I knew Murdock. He—did things like that for Father."

He spoke bitterly. He was without illusions about his father. At some time, when he had found out things first, and the illusions first began to go, he had been bitterly hurt. Now the bitterness was dry and old.

"My dear boy," Laurel Burke said, with a kind of awful archness, "you make Mr. Murdock sound like—what is the word—a pimp. And your father—really, Mr. Merle, I can't have you saying things like that about your dear father."

"You—" Merle began. Then he stopped. His voice grew quieter although his face did not change. "We'll have to talk this over, Miss Burke. We'll have to go into it."

"Of course," Laurel Burke said. "That's why I came. So we could all talk it over like friends."

"Of course," Mr. Potts said gently, "Mr. Merle—Mr. George Merle—was over sixty, wasn't he?"

Laurel Burke looked at him. She said, "Why, Mr. Potts!"

She stood up.

"You know," she said, "I'd really *love* to wash my hands."

They watched her go across the terrace, guided by Meggs, and through one of the French doors. And then they turned and looked at Bill Weigand and waited, the question evident but unphrased. Slowly, with regret, Bill Weigand nodded.

"As I said," he told them, "I am inclined to believe she was your father's girl. The girl he kept. Whether she is going to have a child by him I haven't any idea. Naturally. She may be. If she is, she'll probably be able to collect, unless—"

He paused and looked around at them.

"Unless she killed your father, or was mixed up in it," he said. "Because you may as well know—if you don't know—Murdock didn't kill him. And Murdock didn't kill himself. He didn't, so far as I know, kill anybody. But somebody killed him."

He looked for surprise and found none of it.

"Of course," Mr. Potts said, gently, "we guessed that, Lieutenant. Because otherwise, why would you be here?"

Weigand looked at A. Wickersham Potts and smiled faintly.

"I didn't expect you to be surprised, Mr. Potts," he said.

"Do you think she killed him?" Joshua Merle said, and there was something like hope in his tone.

Weigand shrugged slightly. There was a chance, he said. If, say, he suddenly told her he was finished and that she and the child—if any—could whistle for their support. Then she might have killed, either in rage or with consideration, after weighing one thing against another and deciding that Merle's family was a better bet than Merle. But there was, at the moment, no evidence.

"There are alternatives," he said. "Several alternatives. Miss Burke and Murdock and whatever they had cooked up may have had nothing to do with it."

"You mean," Mr. Potts said, "that there was an understanding between Murdock and Miss Burke—an understanding to defraud Mr. Merle? That he was—a victim?"

Wickersham Potts was shrewd. He was very shrewd. But Weigand contented himself with the non-committal remark that such things happened. In, he pointed out, a variety of ways—variants on the "badger game." Murdock as the outraged husband, for example.

Mr. Potts shook his head. He thought it would not have been that. Knowing George Merle, having met Mr. Murdock, he thought it had not been that. Not in those terms.

"Mr. Merle and Mr. Murdock knew each other quite well," he said. "Much too well for that, I should have thought. But if Mr. Murdock had—found Miss Burke for Mr. Merle and then had arranged with her to share the proceeds of—er—her pregnancy—that would be more likely. And the Mr. and Mrs. Murdock arrangement may not have been so—how shall I say it?—so completely a formality as we are asked to suppose. What do you think of that version, Lieutenant?"

Weigand thought that Mr. Potts was very shrewd indeed, and very observant. It occurred to him that Mr. Potts might some day be too observant for his own good. But he merely said that Mr. Potts's idea was, indeed, an idea.

"It was interesting about the Zero Club," Mr. Potts said. "Very interesting. I don't care for the place, myself. But of course every man to his taste. Don't you all agree?"

Then Mr. Potts got up and went off, not as if he were going any place in particular. And after that, for a long time, Weigand was not sure where Mr. Potts was. He was not, for several hours, sure where anybody was.

There had been a general tendency to break up when Mr. Potts departed; and Mullins, reappearing from the direction of the swimming pool, had looked inquiringly at Bill Weigand. Weigand shook his head. They were not leaving; they were waiting. Because it had occurred to Bill Weigand that it was not so necessary now for him to go to New York. It looked as if the part of New York he was interested in might be coming to Long Island.

He detained Joshua Merle when Merle started to rise, with an "Oh, Mr. Merle. If you've got a moment?" Merle sat down. Weigand's attitude did not encourage the others to remain. Captain Sullivan was already gone; now Stanley Goode and Ann went off together, stopping by the table which held only bottles and glasses again, going together into the shadows of the big living room. Jameson limped off after them, and Joshua Merle's eyes followed him. Bill Weigand's first question brought them back.

"At one time, Mr. Merle," Weigand said, "I gather you knew Mary Hunter—Mary Thorgson she was then—quite well. Is that correct?"

Merle shook his head slightly as if to clear it.

"What's that got to do with it?" he said. "With anything?"

It was, Weigand told him, merely something he wanted to know about; he wanted to know about it because he was investigating a murder—the murder of Mr. Merle's father. Merle was under no obligation to answer, unless he wanted to help.

"I don't get it," Merle said. "Mary doesn't come into this. She—got out fast enough after she got what she wanted. But—yes, I knew her at one time. I thought we were going to get married. Does that surprise you?"

"No," Weigand told him. "What happened?"

"My sainted father," Merle said. "And a check. If you knew Mary and I were engaged, you must have known it from her. But I suppose she didn't tell you all of it. I can see why she wouldn't."

"She told me—she told some friends of mine—that your father intervened," Weigand said.

Intervened, Merle said, was good. Intervened was very good. Weigand waited. Merle said he still didn't see what it had to do with anything, but what the hell?

"I was in love with her," he said. "She acted as if she were in love with me. But Father laughed at that—and he was right that time. He said 'like father, like daughter' and not to trust any Thorgson. You see, her father had tried to gyp the old man once. He didn't get away with it—it was the other way around—but the old boy hated him. Or had contempt for him. And he said Mary was the same breed. I—I suppose I yelled at him. And he just smiled, in a way he had—not a nice way."

The way George Merle smiled meant that he would take care of things in his own fashion, whatever his son thought. He had, Joshua Merle said.

"One afternoon," Merle told Weigand, "the old boy sent for her—I was off changing and she was right here, sitting on this terrace. She went in to see him and when I came out she had gone—with a nice check. It was as easy as that. The old boy said if she wanted money she could get it easier than by marrying me—probably told her some nonsense about cutting me off in his will and stopping my allowance meanwhile. What he called an allowance—enough to keep me in cigarettes and tied to the house. He said he would pay her then and there. And he did. I was worth ten thousand dollars to Mary—ten thousand lousy smackers."

"Did she tell you this?" Weigand asked.

"I didn't see her again," Joshua Merle said. "Not to talk to, anyway. The old boy told me. He was—he was smirking about it. I hated him."

"Yes," Weigand said. "Did you go on hating him, Mr. Merle?"

Merle looked at Bill Weigand and his eyes narrowed.

"I didn't like him much," he said. "I never liked him much after that. But he was right and I suppose he did me a good turn. But I just didn't like him." He paused and looked at Weigand hard. "Do you think I'd kill my father because I didn't like him, Weigand?" he wanted to know.

Weigand shook his head, but did not answer directly. Instead, he asked another question.

"Suppose," he said, "your father lied to you about her. Suppose— I'm merely supposing—he told her some other story—that you had asked him to get rid of her for you. Something like that. And suppose that later, recently say, she found out the story he told you. What would you think of that, Merle?"

Merle thought it was a lot of nonsense. He didn't call it nonsense, but that was roughly what he meant. But after he had said that, he looked at Weigand with narrowed eyes. He wanted, after a moment, to know what Weigand meant by that.

"Your father was killed in Mrs. Hunter's apartment," Weigand said. "Suppose—and this is merely supposition again—she really loved you and never got over it entirely. Suppose she suddenly came into her apartment and found your father there—suppose she arranged to get him there after she found out. Suppose she tried to get him to tell you the truth and he just laughed at her. And suppose all the hate she had been feeling since she found out floated up and—."

Merle looked at Weigand as if he were seeing horrors. He passed his hand over his forehead. It was quite a while before he spoke.

"You're making it up," he said, and swore at Weigand savagely.

Weigand sat quietly and looked at him.

"But I said I was making it up," he agreed. "I said I was supposing. It is a hypothesis entirely, Mr. Merle. Only—it is a possible hypothesis. Assuming your father lied."

"He didn't lie. Not that time," Merle said. He said it with determination, and with anger.

"Oh, yes," Weigand said. "He lied, I think, Mr. Merle. I really think he lied."

He waited and Merle merely stared at the ground.

"You see, Merle," Weigand said, "your father hated Mrs. Hunter's father. He had cheated Mr. Thorgson out of quite a sum of money, I suspect. And often we hate those we wrong—it is a form of self-justification. Your father wasn't going to let Thorgson have the satisfaction of seeing his daughter married to you." Weigand paused. "Of course, to do your father credit," he added, "he may not have thought the feeling between you and Mary was really serious."

Merle did not look up. He spoke to the ground. He said:

"It was serious, all right."

After a considerable time, Merle spoke again.

"Is that all you wanted?" he said.

Weigand agreed it was all he wanted. But when Merle stood up and had taken one limping step, Bill Weigand spoke as if he had just remembered something.

"By the way," he said. "That man who called you at Charles and told you your father had been killed—would you know his voice if you heard it again? Had you ever heard it before?"

"I don't know," Merle said. "I don't remember that I'd ever heard it before. It was muffled, sort of. I didn't think about that—just about what the man said. I just heard what he said and started off without waiting for Jamie."

"Right," Weigand said.

Merle went off. For a man with a limp, he walked fast.

Bill Weigand rather unexpectedly found himself alone. He was alone when Pam and Jerry North arrived, bringing Mary Hunter with them. Then it was a little after four o'clock.

· 11 ·

"Bill," Pam North said, "We found the gun, so we came right out. Because it proves it isn't the gun."

"Oh," Bill Weigand said, "hello, Pam. Jerry. Mrs. Hunter."

"Mrs. Hunter's gun," Jerry North amplified. "It was in the bottom of a trunk in the storage warehouse. She remembered this morning where it ought to be. It never was in the apartment. Pam thought it was important."

Bill said it could be. He held out his hand. Mary Hunter took a .38 revolver out of her handbag and gave it to him. He turned it over and looked at it. It was a nice little gun. There were no cartridges in the cylinder. There was nothing to indicate that it had been used recently; nothing to prove it had not.

"In a trunk in the warehouse," Bill Weigand repeated.

"Yes," Mary Hunter said. "I remembered which trunk I had put it in after Rick went away. Mrs. North thought we ought to get it and bring it to you. We all three went and they watched me take it out of the trunk. Mrs. North thought they'd better, so they could—tell you what they saw."

Bill said that had been the way to do it. He said he would have the gun tested, as a matter of routine.

"You don't seem much interested, Bill," Pam said.

Bill looked at her and smiled. He wanted to know if she had really expected he would be much interested. He said he had no doubt that this gun had been at the bottom of a trunk in a warehouse when George Merle was shot. And that, with the gun found by Murdock's body, they had enough guns. He wondered, but he did not say he wondered, why the Norths had brought Mary Hunter to Elmcroft. Because it was clear they had brought her.

Pam North looked around and said: "Where is everybody?" and Bill Weigand said they were around. Somewhere around. Then he asked a question, suddenly.

"Mrs. Hunter," he said, "did you ever, under any circumstances, for any purpose, accept a check from George Merle? For any purpose—to take to your father, for example; to repay you for an expenditure you had made—for any purpose at all?"

Mary Hunter looked at him and seemed puzzled.

"Why no," she said. "Of course not."

"Right," Bill Weigand said.

"Lieutenant," Mary Hunter said. "Josh didn't hate his father. He hadn't any reason to."

Bill looked sharply at Pam North, who smiled back, quite blandly.

"The only reason Josh could have had for hating his father was because of me," Mary Hunter said. "And Josh didn't—it wasn't serious. Not that serious."

"All right," Bill said. "If you say so."

Mary Hunter said she did say so.

"Mrs. North seemed to think," she said. "Seemed to think you—."

"I merely said it was possible," Pam North said. "I thought if you explained there wouldn't be any confusion. Or if you and Joshua Merle both explained."

"Did you?" Bill Weigand said. "And did you, Jerry?"

"I," Jerry North said, "came along for the ride. At a ruinous expenditure of A coupons, not being a policeman with unlimited rations."

"Well, well," Bill Weigand said. "We'll have to find Mr. Merle presently."

Mullins came from around the house and Mr. Potts was with him. They were talking and seemed to be on very happy terms. Mullins stopped for a moment when he saw the Norths and then, apparently in spite of his wiser instincts, beamed at them. He and Mr. Potts came over and Mr. Potts said "Hello, Mary," before he was introduced to the Norths.

"Why don't you have your friends help themselves to a drink, Lieutenant," Mr. Potts said. He looked informingly at the bar table.

"But—" Pam North said. Jerry took her by the arm and said "Come on, Pam." Mary Hunter hesitated. Then she followed the others. From the living room, Ann Merle came out and joined them. She looked across at Wickersham Potts, who smiled and nodded vigorously.

"Loot," Mullins said, "I don't know if it means anything. But young Merle has been trying to get his sister to marry the Jameson guy. Mr. Potts says so, anyway. He thought you'd want to know."

Potts smiled. He said that the sergeant put it a little more strongly than he would put it. He merely assumed that Lieutenant Weigand would want to know all there was to know about—"about the people in the case."

"Did you?" Weigand said, without committing himself. "Well," Mr. Potts said reasonably, "in your position I would. I would collect all the pieces."

"You have, apparently," Bill Weigand told him.

Potts smiled at Weigand.

"I told you I was interested in people," he said. "I know all these people quite well. I've known them for a number of years, of course."

"Right," Bill said. "And Merle wants his sister to marry Weldon Jameson. I gather she doesn't want to."

"Because of young Goode," Potts added for him. "Of course. No, she doesn't want to. But her brother is insistent—almost insistent."

"And Jameson?" Bill Weigand said.

"Oh," Potts said, "Jameson wouldn't mind. I don't think he'd mind at all." He paused and looked past Weigand into the distance. "A sense of obligation can be a very strange and compelling thing," he said, with a great air of making an abstract remark. "But I mustn't harp on it."

It might, Weigand told Mr. Potts, be helpful if Mr. Potts would say straight out what it was he wanted to say; what he knew or thought he knew. Mr. Potts told him that that was, of course, a very reasonable idea.

"Unfortunately," he said, "I know no facts which would help you." He stopped smiling. "If I did," he said, "I wouldn't beat about the bush. I assure you of that, Lieutenant. I merely have opinions—and guesses. As you must have yourself."

"Why should Merle have a particular sense of obligation to Jameson?" Weigand said. "Because of the plane accident?"

"Oh," Potts said, "Josh won't accept it as an accident. He calls it criminal negligence. His. He thinks he has ruined Jameson's future. Because, you see, Jameson was very intent on flying. He always had been, apparently, since he was a boy. And now he can't. And he hadn't, apparently, made plans for any other kind of life."

The shadow of the house had crept across the flagged terrace and was edging onto the grass beyond. It had grown hot and still on the terrace. Meggs came out again with fresh supplies for the bar table and Bill Weigand, crossing that way with Mullins, decided that it was not formally time for cocktails. Weldon Jameson came out from the living room and poured himself a scotch and his face and eyes showed he had had several before it, although his movements were precise and certain. Meggs mixed Mullins an old-fashioned and Weigand changed to a Tom Collins.

"This is a pretty wet case, ain't it, Loot?" Mullins said.

Jameson limped away toward the swimming pool. Stanley Goode was sitting in the sun by the pool watching Ann Merle, who was back in her white swimming suit and, as Weigand and Mullins watched, dived from the pool's rim.

It was cooler in the living room than on the terrace. Bill Weigand started in and hesitated just outside one of the French doors. Mrs. Burnwood was standing in front of a chair which had its back to Weigand and in which its occupant was hidden.

"—have it," Mrs. Burnwood said rather loudly, and in an angry voice. "You're making him think he owns the place."

She saw Weigand at the door and stopped and looked at him with hostility. She turned and went across the room and out of Weigand's sight. Joshua Merle got up out of the deep chair and came across to the French door. His face was dark and worried. He did not seem to see Weigand until he was almost on him and then he did not pause.

"Still here, Lieutenant?" he said.

There was nothing to say, and Bill Weigand said nothing. Merle turned left on the terrace and went around the house toward, Weigand assumed, the path which led down to the private beach and Potts's cottage. After a few moments, Weigand went after him and had a look. There was no sign of Merle. A graveled path descended in terraces. Weigand went down it and, after a little, came out on a small, immaculate beach. A little way off from the beach was the cottage which was presumably Mr. Potts's. There was no sign of life around, and Bill Weigand went back up the path.

The reaction to his announcement that Murdock had been a victim, not a murderer, was slow in coming. Possibly he had been wrong in thinking it would come. And he needed it—he needed a blowoff. Because it was not enough to know in your own mind; to be pretty sure you knew. Bill went down toward the pool.

Joshua Merle and Mary Hunter met in the living room, with no one else around except Pam North—which was the way Pam had hoped it would happen; to contrive which, Pam had suddenly been overcome with a desire to powder her nose when she saw Merle go in from the terrace and had insisted that Mary Hunter must also want to powder her nose. Jerry had smiled at her and shaken his head a little and then he had joined Mullins at the table which held the drinks.

Mary Hunter had started to turn back when she saw Joshua Merle, tall and angry-looking, but then had straightened and stopped and looked at him. It was a moment before either spoke, and Pam had time to fear that neither was going to speak. Then Joshua Merle said:

"Good afternoon, Mrs. Hunter," as if from a great distance.

"Hello," Mary Hunter said. "Mrs. North brought me here. I—"

"You don't have to tell me you didn't want to come," Merle said. "You made that clear enough a long time ago."

"Josh," Mary Hunter said. "Oh Josh—why—"

That, Pam decided, was her cue. She took it. Neither of them saw her go.

The terrace was deserted. Jerry and Sergeant Mullins were walking across the lawn toward the swimming pool and Laurel Burke was with them—walking between them, with the movements, Pam decided, of a dress model. Pam started to follow them, and resented the necessity of following them—of following anybody—and stopped and said, "Damn!"

"I might as well go home," she thought. "Get Jerry away—get Jerry and go home. Because Mary and Josh have got to work it out themselves from now on. If there is, after all this time and Rick Hunter and everything, anything to work out."

"Oh," a gentle voice said, "I think there is, Mrs. North. I think you were very wise to bring Mrs. Hunter out."

"I often talk out loud," Pam said to Wickersham Potts. "Don't pay any attention to me. I've tried not to, but there it is. I suppose it wasn't any of my business, really."

"No," Mr. Potts said, "speaking strictly—I suppose not. But one's business is so limited if one sticks to it too religiously. Mine, for example, is playing an organ." He paused to consider. "Which I play extremely well," he added. "Probably as well as anyone in this country. You've heard me, perhaps?"

"Oh, yes," Pam said. "It was very fine. Only I suppose I don't really appreciate the pipe organ, Mr. Potts. Not that it isn't—tremendous."

"I also play the flute," Mr. Potts said. "For my own amusement. A flute is much more amusing than an organ. But, of course, limited. But even an organ does not occupy a whole life. Not even mine."

"No," Pam said. "Do you think, too, that Mary and Josh ought to explain things? Quit misunderstanding each other? Just—just because it is so foolish to let an old lie—it was a lie, I suppose."

"Oh, yes," Mr. Potts said. "Dear old George was a very intelligent liar, when he wanted to be. And he often wanted to be. You see, he

hated Mary's father. So he—eliminated Mary. He often eliminated
people. On the other hand, he contributed very handsomely to the
church and so helped pay my salary." He considered. "I don't know
that that strikes a balance, entirely," he said. "But there it is."

"And he got himself murdered," Pam said. "There that is, too."

"Oh," Mr. Potts said, "do you think there is a connection? I rather
thought—but no doubt you are right." He considered again. "At any
rate," he said, "in the sense that everything is connected with something else. In the end."

Pam said that that was what she had meant. Then she spoke suddenly.

"Do you know who killed Mr. Merle, Mr. Potts?" she said.

Wickersham Potts looked at her, and she thought afterward that his
eyes had narrowed slightly.

"Oh, yes," he said. "Of course. Don't you?"

"I'm not sure," Pam said. "I think I do."

"Of course," Mr. Potts said, "we can both be wrong. There are so
many side issues. And it is so difficult to tell which *is* a side issue.
Miss Burke and her baby, if there is a baby. Mr. Murdock and his murder, if he was murdered."

"Oh," Pam said, "he was murdered."

Mr. Potts nodded.

"Mary Hunter and Josh," he said. "And, of course, the money—all
the money. And the smallness of young Merle's allowance. And the
accident which kept him out of the Navy. It is really very complex."

They were still standing near the French doors. Potts looked around
them.

"All this," he said, "it's quite impressive, isn't it. Have you seen my
little place? Really, it's the Merles' little place too, but they let me rent
it. For years now."

"No," Pam said.

"I'd like you to," Mr. Potts said. "Would you care to?"

"Why yes," Pam said. "Very much, Mr. Potts."

And that was not really accurate. But she did want, quite a good
deal, to know why Mr. Potts wanted her to see his little place.

Mr. Potts directed her down the terraced path toward the beach, and up the other path from the beach to the cottage. He pushed open the door and she went in ahead of him. The living room was large for a place which seemed, from outside, so tiny—it was large and underfurnished with chairs and tables which seemed light and clean. It was a room beautifully, miraculously, free of clutter.

"Mr. Potts," she began, when she heard footsteps behind her, "it's—"

And then, blindingly, without warning, her head pained with incredible, flaring violence and blackness came in from the sides as she felt herself falling. She spent the remaining moment of consciousness thinking that this was very odd of Mr. Potts, and very unlike him.

Her head ached as she had never known it to ache, in great swirls of pain. She tried to raise herself from the polished floor against which her cheek was pressed and the pain hurled her down. She lay for a moment and the pain was less intense and she pushed herself up to sit on the floor, holding herself up with her hands thrust out in front of her. She shook her head, and the pain came back, but she could remember more clearly.

Mr. Potts had asked her to come to see his cottage, and she had thought he wanted to tell her something. And he had let her precede him into the cottage and there had been footsteps behind her as she was admiring the room and—

She was looking at blood. A little rivulet of blood, like spilled water but less fluid, was creeping across the polished boards in front of her. As she looked it stopped creeping; it was a red finger of blood, motionless on the floor.

Pam North made herself turn. Wickersham Potts lay a few feet away from her. He lay on his face. The blood was coming up around a knife in his back.

Pam fought back the blackness which came up around her. She pushed at it desperately with her will, but her will was not strong enough. Darkness engulfed her again and she pitched forward onto the floor. One of her hands, as she lay huddled on the floor, was an inch or two from the finger of blood which pointed away from Wickersham

Potts, late organist of St. Andrew's, amateur in human behavior; Mr. Potts, who in the end had encountered a professional.

Jerry North and Bill Weigand found Pam and she was still unconscious. She regained consciousness in Jerry's arms and looked up at him and said, "Hello, darling. What happened?" before she remembered what had happened. Then she turned her face and pressed it against Jerry's arm and he held it there. Without moving, her words muffled, she said: "Mr. Potts, Jerry. He's dead, isn't he?"

"Yes," Jerry said.

Pam lifted her head, but she did not look at the body.

"He was such a nice little man, Jerry," she said. "At first I thought he hit me. I couldn't see why."

Bill Weigand stood up beside Potts's body. He said that, if she felt up to it, it would help for her to tell what happened. Jerry said, "For God's sake, Bill!" But Pam sat up, still in the circle of Jerry's arm, and said she was all right. She still did not look at the body.

She told them of coming to the cottage with Mr. Potts, of hearing footsteps behind her and of being struck. As she remembered, she put her hand up and touched the back of her head gently.

"It's all right, Pam," Jerry said. "Just a bump. A pretty big bump. He didn't try to kill you. You were just—in the way."

Pam smiled at Jerry to reassure him. Her smile quivered a little.

"I thought Mr. Potts hit me," she said. "But then I knew he didn't."

"When you came to," Bill said. "And then fainted again. I gather you must have, because you knew he was dead."

"I think I did," Pam said. "It's blurred. But before that, I knew it wasn't Mr. Potts."

"How, Pam?" Jerry said. "Did you see him?"

But Pam shook her head, slowly, bewildered.

"I don't think so," she said. "That's all blurred too. I don't think I saw anybody—except Mr. Potts, of course. But I just remember thinking 'why, it isn't Mr. Potts at all' while I was falling. The first time, that must have been. Because the second time it was Mr. Potts, of course. Only it's all mixed up."

"Never mind," Jerry said. "It will come straight."

"If it does," Pam said, "I'll know who it was—I mean, who it was all the time. Mr. Merle and Mr. Murdock and now Mr. Potts—I'll know the whole thing."

And as she said that an odd feeling came over her. It was a cold, unhappy feeling; it was like the feeling of a great disappointment.

They started out, Pam a little shaky even with Jerry's supporting arm about her. When they were at the door, Bill Weigand turned back suddenly and went to the body. Gently he turned it so he could see the face. There was no doubt about it. Mr. Potts looked, in death, very surprised indeed.

Most of them were back on the terrace when Bill Weigand and the Norths reached the top of the terraced path and came around the house. Weigand counted them up as they walked toward them—Joshua Merle and Mary, sitting side by side; Weldon Jameson and Stanley Goode sitting in a little group of which Ann Merle was the third; Laurel Burke with Mullins close to her, as he was supposed to be; Captain Theodore Sullivan of the State Police, by himself. Meggs at the table mixing drinks. Mrs. Burnwood—no Mrs. Burnwood.

Weldon Jameson started up as he saw them coming. He said, "Mrs. North! You're hurt!" and started toward them.

"She's all right, Mr. Jameson," Bill Weigand said. "She—bumped her head."

"How—?" Ann Merle began, but Bill stopped her.

"I'm going to tell you," he said, and his voice was distant and level. "All of you. Meggs!"

Meggs came across the terrace.

"Ask Mrs. Burnwood to come out," Weigand told him. Meggs said, "Yes, sir," and went into the living room. They waited. After a few minutes Mrs. Burnwood came out and looked at Weigand without cordiality.

"You sent for me?" she inquired, as if she were expressing an impossibility. "You *sent* for me?"

"Yes," Bill told her. "Please sit down, Mrs. Burnwood."

She looked very surprised. She sat down.

"Now," Bill Weigand said, still standing. "One of you stabbed Mr. Potts in the back within the last half hour. You were very successful. You killed him. Before that, the same person slugged Mrs. North and knocked her out. I don't know why whoever it was didn't kill her, too, but apparently that wasn't the intention."

"Wicky?" Ann said. "Not Wicky?"

"No, no," Mrs. Burnwood said. Nobody else said anything for a moment and Captain Sullivan stood up. Bill Weigand nodded.

"Yes, Captain," he said. "Your bailiwick, definitely. In the cottage down by the beach."

Sullivan went among the chairs, striding, and around the corner of the house.

"The poor little guy," Laurel Burke said. Then she stood up suddenly. "Listen," she said, and her voice was no longer artfully deep. "I'm getting out of here. The hell out of here."

"No," Bill told her. "Nobody's getting out of here. Not now."

"But," she said.

"Nobody," Weigand repeated. "Captain Sullivan will want you all here. Until he takes over, I want you all here."

"Really, Lieutenant," Mrs. Burnwood said. "Really. You speak as if—" then she stopped and her eyes were surprised.

"Right," Bill Weigand said. "That's just the way I speak. One of you—one of you here—killed Mr. Potts. Also Mr. Merle and Murdock. Mr. Potts, because he knew which one of you killed Merle. Is that clear enough?"

"Too damned clear," Jameson said. "And Potts did know. He told me he knew."

Weigand had a hunch and played it.

"I think," he said, "that he told each person here that he knew the identity of the murderer. He was—playing a little game."

"It was a damned dangerous game," Joshua Merle said.

Weigand nodded.

"Yes, Mr. Merle," he said. "It was a very dangerous game. Because, you see, he did know. And the murderer knew he knew. To one of you he said something more than he did to the others—too much more."

"But," Ann said, and her voice was doubtful, "how could he know? He was here all day yesterday. I'm sure of that."

Weigand nodded.

"Right," he said. "As far as evidence went, I don't think Mr. Potts could prove anything. But I think he knew, just the same—for a very simple reason. He knew all of you very well—he was very interested in people. He knew things—little things and big things—which it would take an outsider years to learn. Among the big things he knew was the identity of the person who killed Mr. Merle."

· 12 ·

WEDNESDAY, 7:15 P.M. TO 9:05 P.M.

Lieutenant Weigand made a little dot with his pencil after each of the names on the sheet of paper before him. He looked at the names and the little dots and then he looked across the desk which had been George Merle's and shook his head at Captain Theodore Sullivan of the Criminal Identification Division of the State Police.

"So," Sullivan said. "It isn't very helpful, Lieutenant."

It wasn't, Weigand agreed, helpful at all. It left them where they had started. No one admitted having been near the beach cottage at around ten minutes to six, which was, as nearly as they could reconstruct it, the time Pam North was slugged. Everyone was sure that he was somewhere else—and no one could prove that he was somewhere else. Mary Hunter and Joshua Merle had been talking then—or about then. They had not particularly noticed the time. But about that time—they thought without conviction that it was a little later—they had parted and Merle had gone in search of Weldon Jameson. He said he merely "wanted to talk to Jameson." He had, by his own account, been unsuccessful in finding Jameson. Mary Hunter had sat where he left her. "I just sat there. I wasn't thinking about the time. I didn't care what time it was!"

It did not sound, Weigand thought, as if there had been the reconciliation between the two that Pam North had expected—that had, he guessed, brought the Norths and Mary with them to Elmcroft. Why, he wondered, had there been no reconciliation? The presumptive reason was that neither believed the other—or that one did not believe the other—when they talked, as surely they had talked, of that summer afternoon two years earlier when George Merle had called a girl who looked very young in a white play dress into his study and looked at her coldly across the desk. This desk—Weigand's fingers tapped it.

He thought he knew the answer to the question he had to answer. One stuck out, unreconcilably. But if he did not know the answer—if that discrepancy *could* be reconciled—then any continuing antagonism between Mary Hunter and Joshua Merle might be interesting.

He put that aside, and returned to his list. Jameson—and his pencil hovered over the name as he recapitulated for himself and Captain Sullivan—had not been able to understand why Josh Merle could not find him. He had been in plain sight. Or, if he had not actually been in plain sight from all angles, he had certainly not been hard to find. He had been sitting, he said, in a deck chair down by the pool, his back to the terrace—hidden from the terrace, no doubt, by the canvas of the chair. But from the pool, he told the detectives, he had been in plain enough sight for anyone. He had seen no one by the pool.

Laurel Burke had been, she indicated, practically everywhere. "Just looking around," she told them with a certain emphasis. "Just sizing things up, Miss Burke?" Sullivan had asked her, and she had smiled at him without answering. She had been through as much of the house as she could get through unobtrusively, which seemed to mean that she had not actually forced locked doors. She had been down by the pool, but she did not remember that she had seen Jameson there. But she did not remember that she had not seen him there.

"I wasn't looking for Donny," she said, and corrected herself quickly. "For Mr. Jameson."

The point was interesting, and they went into it. She stuck for a little while to the argument that she had merely used a nickname—a nickname she thought appropriate—facetiously. But after only a little questioning she gave that argument up as hardly worth the trouble.

Very well, she had known Weldon Jameson before. Very slightly. She
had met him one night at a night club when she was there with Murdock. No, not with George Merle. Yes, Jameson had a girl with him.
No, she had never seen the girl before—or since. She was a—

"—oh, a Miss Jones for all I know," she said. "What did I care who
she was. I'd heard about Mr. Jameson, of course—I knew him—he
was a guest at Mr. Merle's. And Murdock knew him and he and the
girl came over. We all had a few drinks and the girl called him Donny.
So I called him Donny."

"That," Sullivan said, "doesn't wash, Miss Burke."

"Doesn't it," she said, with only a mockery of polite interest. "So
what?"

There was no immediate answer to that one, but it was still one to
be answered. They put Miss Burke aside.

Mrs. Burnwood had gone to her room to lie down. She had locked
the door behind her—"to keep out intruders," she explained, a little
balefully—and she had lain down. She had got up again and been
ready to come down when Weigand sent for her. Her voice curled
reproachfully over the word "sent." She assumed she had been lying
down from around five thirty until after six. She couldn't prove it.

"None of them," Sullivan pointed out, "can prove anything."

"Right," Weigand said. "A disability they share with us."

"Yeah," Sullivan said.

Not even Ann Merle and Stanley Goode had been together uninter-
ruptedly through any period which certainly covered the time of the
attack on Pam North and the killing of Wickersham Potts. Ann had
seen her aunt go into the house, had thought she looked distraught, and
had gone after her to see whether there was anything she could do. She
had arrived just as her aunt turned the key in the lock. She had decided
there was nothing she could do; she had stopped by her room to redo
her hair and when she went back to the terrace, Stanley Goode was no
longer there. He had come out of the house a few minutes later—how
many minutes, what time it was then—those things were anybody's
guess. Ann's guess was that it was a little before six.

Goode had sat for a few minutes after Ann left him and then had gone to a lavatory in the house. He had been gone perhaps ten minutes, come back and found Ann still missing, had sauntered down toward the pool and then had discovered that he had left his watch in the lavatory where he washed his hands. He went back and got the watch and came out again, this time finding Ann.

"And what time was it by your watch?" Weigand wanted to know.

Goode looked at him and shrugged.

"Personally," Weigand commented to Sullivan, "I never put a watch on without noticing what time it is, do you?"

"I don't know," Sullivan said. "I never thought about it. Probably not."

Jerry North had been talking with Mullins, had had a drink or two with Mullins, standing somewhere near the bar, and then had suddenly become convinced that he had left the car ignition turned on. He had gone out to the car circle to look.

"And had you, Jerry?" Bill Weigand asked.

"No," Jerry said. "Of course not. But, as Pam would say, it's a thing like leaving the water turned on. Or the oven going. You know better, but there you are."

He had come back and Mullins was gone.

"With me," Sullivan explained, at that point. "We—we went out and looked at the garden."

"Why, for God's sake?" Bill Weigand asked him.

"I like gardens," Sullivan explained simply. "So does the sergeant. Didn't you know?"

"No," Weigand said. "He lives in Brooklyn."

"He still likes gardens," Sullivan said. "So we went to look at the Merles'—it's down beyond the pool."

"Right," Bill said. "How is it?"

"It needs water," Sullivan said. He reflected. "All gardens always need water," he added.

Weigand finished his list and looked at Sullivan. He said you would think that, with so many people around, some two of them—excepting Mullins and Sullivan himself—would have been together. You'd think somebody would have known what time it was.

"Why?" Sullivan said. "What time is it now? Without looking."

"About seven thirty," Weigand said, without looking. Then he looked. It was seven twenty-eight.

"All right," Sullivan said. "Have it your own way. But these people didn't."

"Or," Bill told him, "they say they didn't. For reasons of their own."

There was, Sullivan agreed, always that. He asked Weigand what the discrepancy was, and Weigand, with enough background to make it comprehensible, told him. Sullivan thought about it and nodded. He said maybe it would do the trick but that he'd hate to go to court on it. He wanted to know the motive, and Bill Weigand told him that—guessed at that for him. Sullivan said he still wouldn't want to go to court.

"My God," Bill said, with some irritability. "Do you think that if I had a case to take to court I wouldn't make the pinch? Do you think I'd be waiting for another move out of our murderer?"

Pam North leaned back in the lounge chair on the terrace, her head turned toward Jerry sitting beside her. This was partly so she could look at Jerry, but it was largely because there was a tender bump on the back of her head. Her head ached a little, but not too insistently. She sipped a long rum collins and her mind went around and around. It was worse than the headache.

"Think, Jerry," she directed. "What kinds of things are there?"

"Sounds," Jerry told her. "Smells. Touch—did you touch something? Involuntarily—the clothing of the person who struck you? Did you feel—oh, say heavy rough tweed—and identify somebody who was wearing a tweed jacket?"

"Nobody is," Pam told him. "Nobody's wearing any jacket at all."

It was, Jerry told her, merely an example.

"It would," Pam said, "be a much better example in October. Anyway, it's an obvious example. This must have been more subtle, like—oh, the dampness of a bathing suit."

"What?" Jerry said. "What's subtle about a damp bathing suit?"

The way she meant it, Pam said, there might be a lot. Because there might be a dampness—a coolness—to be felt by merely being a few inches away from a damp bathing suit, even without touching it.

"That," she explained, "would be extremely subtle, I think."

"Well," Jerry said, "was it that?"

Pam looked at him in surprise. She said of course not. She said it was merely an example. "Like," she said, "a brown and green jacket out of very heavy tweed. Like one in—"

"No," Jerry said, firmly. "I don't like women in tweed. So don't tell me where one was."

She smiled at him. She said tweed wore forever, but all right.

"As a matter of fact," she said, "I don't think it was—what is the word?—at all."

"Tactile," Jerry told her. "If you don't know what it was you can't remember about the person who hit you, and by which you could identify him or her if you could remember, how do you know it wasn't tactile. Or tactual."

"Jerry!" Pam said. "Are you all right?"

"Perfectly," Jerry said. "How, Pam?"

"Because," Pam said, "it doesn't—oh, feel right. It doesn't feel as if it were something I'd touched. Maybe it was a smell or a sound. I'll just have to wait for it to come back. Only—and this is odd—I have a feeling of dread that it will come back. What do you think that means, Jerry?"

Jerry said he was afraid it meant that whatever it was she could not remember would, when she remembered it, identify somebody she liked as the person who had killed Potts.

"And," Pam said, feeling her bump, "hit me. I hope not."

There was a considerable pause, while both sipped their drinks. Then Jerry said, idly, that something would happen to bring it back to her.

"You'll hear something," he said, "or smell something or taste something and it will all come back to you. Things do."

"Well," Pam said, "I'm almost sure I didn't taste anybody. There wasn't time and anyway—but probably you're right. Probably the condition—whatever it was—will repeat itself and then—" She broke off and sipped again. Then, suddenly, she sat up.

"Jerry!" she said. "I can't. You know I can't. Because Bill doesn't know and if we just *sit* whoever it is will do it again. Because somebody else knows, or because he wasn't through the first time and needs another murder to make things come straight. I've got to try to *bring* it back, whatever it was."

She couldn't, Jerry told her, do it that way. She couldn't force it. Pam listened and shook her head. She said she could try.

"How?" Jerry wanted to know.

"I can smell people, to start with," Pam said. "I can smell everybody here."

Jerry said, "Pam!" and started up, but she was up before him and when he started to go with her she made furious motions of negation. He would spoil everything, the gestures meant, and when he still hesitated, she came close and whispered with great emphasis:

"Jerry!" she whispered. "*Two* people can't go around smelling people."

A little weakly, after that, Gerald North sat down. He consoled himself that most of the others were on the terrace and that Pam, even while engaged in smelling them, would be in plain sight. It also occurred to Jerry that never before had he seen anybody going around and smelling other people, with malice aforethought.

There were four people at the next table and Pam started, because he was nearest, with Stanley Goode. She hesitated a moment behind him, evidently uncertain how to go about it, and decided—it appeared to her fascinated and somewhat awed husband—on the direct approach. She simply leaned over and sniffed Mr. Goode, rather as if he were a piece of doubtful meat.

Ann Merle, who was sitting to the right of Goode, looked at Pam North and shook her head slightly and blinked. The light, although the sun was setting and the shadow was now far out on the lawn, was good enough for Jerry to see her blink. Stanley Goode also saw her blink and looked at her inquiringly. He also, Jerry thought, looked as if he were uneasy. Apparently being smelled had the same effect on a sensitive person as being stared at. It made them feel something was wrong.

Pam, who had evidently not noticed Ann Merle's surprised observation, leaned over and sniffed again. Then she stood up, apparently to consider the odor.

"What?" Stanley Goode said suddenly. "Did you—who is—what?"

Apparently, Jerry decided, Pam must have sniffed audibly.

"What?" Pam said, with quick presence of mind. "Did you say something, Mr. Goode?"

Mr. Goode shook his head slightly, in a puzzled sort of way.

"No," he said. "Oh, Mrs. North. I thought you said something."

"Me?" Mrs. North said. "I?"

"I," Ann Merle said, a little darkly, "thought so too, Mrs. North."

"No," Pam said. "I didn't say anything. What would I say?"

"It sounded," Stanley Goode said, "as if you said, 'Uh, uh' in a whisper."

"Why no," Pam said, "why would I say 'uh, uh.' I mean—is it a joke, or something? I mean, I was just—just walking around." She looked at Stanley Goode, and Jerry North could imagine that her eyes were round and surprised. "I don't say 'uh, uh' when I'm just walking around," Pam pointed out. She paused and considered. "If ever," she said. She put her head up, as she waited for an answer to that one, and it occurred to Jerry that she was sniffing again, in plain sight this time. She seemed to have her nose trained on Ann Merle.

"Oh," Stanley Goode said. "I seem to—I seem to have got things mixed up. I'm sorry, Mrs. North."

"Oh," Pam said, "that's all right. It might happen to anyone."

That, Jerry decided, was an exaggeration. What had just happened to Stanley Goode was not really likely to happen to anyone.

Pam moved on and Jerry, fascinated, got up and moved on behind her. To all appearances, he hoped, they were merely sauntering. Pam moved on to Mary Hunter, who sat at the left of Stanley Goode, and hardly paused. Apparently, Jerry decided, she already knew what Mary Hunter smelled like. Jerry tried to remember and succeeded—she smelled of a Chanel, not No. 5. Very pleasantly. Jerry, as he thought this, came up behind Stanley Goode, and as he did so he felt a disturbing compulsion coming over him—an alarming curiosity. What *did*

Stanley Goode smell like? Before he had time to stop himself, Jerry
North realized he had to find out.

Alarmed at himself, but quite unable to do anything about it, Jerry
North found himself approaching Stanley Goode from behind, a little
as if he were stalking him. Mr. Goode, already somewhat unnerved,
apparently felt his approach, because when Jerry was still a stride or
two away he moved his shoulders a little nervously and started to turn.
There was only one thing to do, and Jerry North did it. He advanced
resolutely and clapped Stanley Goode heartily on the shoulder, at the
same time bending over him in what must be, Jerry fleetingly realized,
a rather awful parody of extreme friendliness.

"How are you, old man?" Mr. North demanded, heartily, using of
all locutions that which he always, in his rational moments, found
most offensive.

Stanley Goode jumped convulsively under his hand. He said,
"What!" in a sudden, loud voice and started up. Then he said, "Oh,"
and sat down again. But he sat tentatively, and he looked around at
Gerald North with disturbed surprise. "All right, I guess," he said.
"Why?"

"That's good," Jerry said, with a kind of horrible heartiness.
"Well—be seeing you."

Pam had passed, and no doubt smelled Joshua Merle, who made the
fourth at the table. Jerry, staggering a little with embarrassment, went
after her.

Stanley Goode smelled of tobacco, some kind of talcum and rye
whiskey. Ann Merle smelled of some kind of flower toilet water and
hardly at all of rum. Jerry did not stop to smell Joshua Merle—never,
he told himself, would he smell anybody again if he could help it. It
was the sort of thing which led to misunderstandings. Jerry paused at
that thought. He decided, after the pause, that misunderstanding was
the best thing it could possibly lead to. It might, it occurred to him,
lead to understanding, which would obviously be worse.

Pam had gone to join Weldon Jameson at the bar. She was standing
much closer to him than she usually stood to other men than Jerry, and
even from a distance Jerry thought he could detect her nose vibrating

delicately. Jerry found he was near a chair and, with a small groan, he sat in it. He sat in it and wished it would get dark.

He was still sitting in the same chair half an hour later when Pam found him. She sat down on the grass behind him and looked at him thoughtfully.

"Well," she said, "I smelled everybody. Mr. Goode and Ann and Mary and Mr. Merle and Mr. Jameson and the Burke girl—my!"

"Yes," Jerry said.

"Just 'my'," Pam told him. "Something very remarkable—something people would call 'Torrid Night' or something. And gin of course."

She paused and thought.

"Of course," she said, "everybody smells of something to drink, which is confusing. Mrs. Burnwood smells of sachet, lavender sachet. Isn't that nice?"

"Is it?" Jerry said. "I never thought so, particularly."

"Well," Pam said, "maybe 'appropriate' is better than nice. It was a very correct way for her to smell. And she hardly smelled of anything to drink at all."

"And—" Jerry began, and then Bill Weigand came up. He sat down on the other side of Pam.

"And what," Bill said in a considered tone, "have you been up to, Pam? You've been talking to everybody here, and standing close to them and, so far as I could tell, feeling the material in their clothes. Is it—a new game or something?"

"She's been smelling them, too," Jerry said. "She's smelled everybody on the place, except you."

"Oh," Pam said. "I smelled him, too. He's tobacco, chiefly."

Bill Weigand looked at them, and shook his head slowly. He waited. Pam told him. He was amused, but he was not wholly amused.

"If I saw you," he pointed out, "other people saw you. They may have wondered, too, what you were up to. One person may have wondered a great deal."

Pam shook her head. She said it was because Bill knew her, and she wasn't acting as he expected her to act. To people who didn't know her, she probably seemed perfectly normal.

"Really," she said, "I made it all look like nothing at all, unless you were looking for something."

Somebody among those present, Bill pointed out, was looking for something. That was precisely it. Somebody was looking for anything—somebody was seeing suspicion in every movement, somebody was starting each time leaves rustled in a breeze; somebody had the wary watchfulness of the hunted.

"And," Jerry said, "if you really think you didn't look as if you were up to something, Pam—well."

"By the way," Pam said, "I didn't know you knew Mr. Goode, Jerry. Not well enough to—hit him."

"What?" Bill said.

Pam looked at Jerry, who looked back at her.

"Oh," Pam said, "nothing. Just a little joke—a little family joke."

Bill Weigand did not look as if he believed either of them, but he let it lie.

"Well," he said, "since you did do it—did you find out anything? Was it an odor—or the sound of a voice—or the feel of something?"

Pam shook her head slowly.

"I don't know," she said. "Things came back. Mrs. Burnwood's sachet made me remember a rainy day when I was a little girl and I was playing with the sewing machine and the belt came off. And Laurel Burke made me remember the opening of an awful play with an ocelot in it, because the woman who sat next to me smelled like that. And Weldon Jameson's coat—he is wearing a coat now, Jerry—made me remember something not very clear about a boy and an ice cream cone. And—and that sort of thing. But nothing made me remember anything more about the person who hit me and killed Mr. Potts."

She paused and looked at Jerry first and then at Bill.

"Only," she said, "something brought it nearer. Not enough nearer—just a little nearer."

"Good," Jerry said. "What was it?"

"I don't know," Pam said. "It was sort of—sort of delayed. And then I couldn't remember what it was. But I don't think it was a smell."

She paused again.

"It's very exasperating," she said. "It's just on the tip of my mind."

Jerry told her to forget it. He told her that it would come back most quickly if she didn't try to force it; he told her, urgently, that Bill was right—that whoever was being hunted was alert and uneasy; that anything she did which was odd, which forced the issue, might frighten him into violence. And that if it did, she might be in the path of the violence.

"After all," Jerry said with finality. "Once is enough. You've been knocked out for getting in the way. For God's sake, darling, stay out of the way!"

"But—" Pam started, and this time Bill Weigand interrupted her.

"Anyway, Pam," he said, "I know—I'm pretty sure I know."

"Who?" Pam said.

Bill Weigand shook his head. He said not yet. He shook his head again when Pam asked why, if he knew, he did not arrest whoever it was.

"Because," he said, "I haven't a shadow of a case. I've a discrepancy—and a hunch." He smiled at her. "Neither of which," he said firmly, "am I going to share with you, my dear. Because probably you would go up and ask him—or her—why he did it, and that might make him mad." He paused and smiled again. "Or her mad," he added. "And we don't want a murderer mad at you, Pam—not this time."

It was almost dark, and for an hour Pam North had been going over the case in her mind, looking for the discrepancy. She had not found it and Jerry had not been helpful. She had taken up, one after another, the people involved in the case and she had tried to remember all that they had said—all that Bill had told her they had said and all that she remembered—and nothing had come out.

It was not that she lacked theories—she had an overabundance of theories. She had a theory to fit Joshua Merle and another to fit Mary Hunter and yet another, which she liked even less, to fit them both together—a theory which involved conspiracy, and pretense of estrangement and murder for money. It was a theory which she could not flatly disprove; it was also a theory in which she could not believe, because she did not think it fitted the people. But there was always a chance that the people did not fit what she thought about them.

It was easier to imagine that Laurel Burke was the murderer, if you granted her remarkable effrontery, because only remarkable effrontery would explain her pushing herself—as she was pushing herself—into the middle of things when she might as easily have remained outside them. It was not possible at all to imagine Ann Merle as the one they were looking for because Ann Merle seemed outside so much of it. "But of course," Pam told herself, "that is really because I've just met her, so naturally I feel that she has just come in. But really she has been in all her life. It's all a matter of perspective."

"Jerry," Pam said, "have you gone to sleep? And where is everybody?"

"No," he said. "But I thought you had. I thought you were all tired out from smelling people and had gone to sleep. Everybody's around some place. Bill and Sullivan are down at the cottage, with a lot of other State cops. As a matter of fact, you must have been asleep."

"No," Pam said. "Anyway, not much. Why don't we go home?"

"I don't know," Jerry said. He had got a waterproof cushion shaped like a wedge and was leaning against it, with a glass in his hand. "Why don't we go home?"

Pam did not answer him. It was not dark yet, but the sun was far down and the shadow was almost at the swimming pool. The light was fading slowly, as if it had all summer to fade in.

"What was the discrepancy, Jerry?" Pam said. "Bill's discrepancy?"

"Something about the check?" Jerry said. "Something about the gun? I don't know."

Jerry spoke as if he, like the light, had all summer to fade in, and were going about it in a leisurely fashion. He spoke as if he were thinking about something else.

"Jerry!" Pam said. "How many drinks have you had?"

"I don't know," Jerry said. "About the right amount."

Pam reached over with her foot and kicked him gently. He said, "Hey!" but not as if it really mattered. Pam asked him again where everybody was.

"Ann and her tennis player went off somewhere," he said. "Down by the pool, probably. And Mary went down that way too, about half an hour ago, when you were sleeping. About Jameson I don't know, unless he's paired off with the Burke." He paused, took a drink and reflected. "Which wouldn't be healthy, I shouldn't think," he said after he had swallowed.

"Healthy?" Pam repeated and Jerry said, "Yes, healthy."

"Because," he said, "either she killed Merle, in which case she isn't a healthy person to be around, or she didn't. In which case she still isn't a healthy person to be around. She knew Jameson before, you know."

"Jerry," Pam said. "How did you know? I mean—how did *you* know?"

Jerry sat up and looked at her and said, "Really, Pam," and said that of course he knew—or guessed. "Even before Bill told me," he said. "She was talking at him when she lugged in the Zero Club."

"Why?" Pam wanted to know. "Why was she talking at him? She was talking at anybody. At everybody."

"Intuition," Jerry told her. "My intuition. Masculine intuition. Or did you think there wasn't any?"

Pam said of course she didn't think there wasn't any. She said everybody had intuition and that it didn't matter about sex. Jerry looked up at her and she said that he knew perfectly well what she meant. She said he was always catching her up when he knew perfectly well she was already up.

"My intuition usually consists in understanding you," Jerry said. "I'll give you that."

"Intuition," Pam said, "merely consists in not going around Robin Hood's barn. It's not taking all the steps. Which doesn't mean that the steps aren't there. They're understood. Like nouns."

"What?" Jerry said.

"Like nouns," Pam said. "Anyway, I think it was nouns. The noun is understood. Or was it the verb? In grammar."

Jerry said he didn't know.

"Anyway," Pam said, "that's what intuition is. Yours or anybody's. It's merely taking a short cut through the woods because you've already been around by the road and know the way. You knew it was Jameson that Burke was talking at because you've seen people talk at people and you know how it looks and sounds. So when you saw it again you took a short cut through the woods instead of going around the barn. Why Robin Hood's, incidentally?"

Jerry said he didn't know.

"Well, anyway," said Pam, who was sitting up now and even leaning forward a little so she could look at Jerry. "That's how you knew it was Jameson. It's perfectly simple."

Jerry said, "Oh."

"Perfectly," Pam said. "Only of course you were wrong. You got lost in the woods somewhere. If it was anybody, it was Josh Merle. Only I'm not sure it was anybody. I think she was just fishing."

"Fishing?" Jerry said. "For what?"

That, Pam said, she did not know. Any more than she knew what it was she remembered, but had forgotten, about the person who struck her and killed Mr. Potts.

"It's very exasperating," she said. "Here Bill knows and if I could remember we'd know too, or if we could work it out the way he did."

"We could use intuition," Jerry said.

Pam shook her head. She said that Bill hadn't used intuition, or at least she didn't think he had.

There were footsteps on the flagstones behind them and the footsteps ended and Stanley Goode came across the grass toward them, the sound of his steps lost in the grass. He stopped and he spoke lightly. He asked if they had happened to notice where Ann Merle had got to. And then he looked down at Pam and seemed surprised at the response to his question.

The response was unquestionably surprising. Pam North did not answer—she did not speak at all. But she looked at him with eyes which grew round and startled and it seemed to Jerry, watching her, that something had happened which to Pam was frightening. He started to speak, but then Pam spoke instead.

"Mr. Goode!" she said. "Did you walk across the terrace just now? The—the hard part? The flagstones?"

"Why," Stanley Goode said, and his words came slowly and the note in his voice was odd. "Yes, I guess I did. I came from the living room, so I must have walked across the terrace. Why, Mrs. North?"

"Oh," Pam said. "So that—" She broke off. "I'm afraid I don't know where Ann went, Mr. Goode," she said. "I thought she was with you."

Pam stood up as she spoke and Jerry, not knowing precisely why, stood with her. He was surprised, but pleased, when she put her hand in his.

"Perhaps she's down by the pool, Mr. Goode," Pamela North said, very politely. "Perhaps you would find her if you looked down there."

Mr. Goode looked no less puzzled, but he accepted the change in Pamela North with politeness. He said that that was a jolly good idea and that he would go down and have a look. He went off, not hurrying, and Pam waited a moment before her grip on Jerry's hand tightened and she was pulling him toward the terrace.

"Jerry," she said. "Jerry! We've got to hurry!"

"Hurry?" Jerry said. "Hurry where, Pam?"

"Anywhere," Pam said. "Where everybody is. We've got to find people, Jerry. Because if we don't it will be Mr. Murdock all over again."

She started off. Jerry held her a moment. He told her, not quite as a question, that now she knew.

"Of course," she said. "Of course." She was impatient.

"But," Jerry said, "apparently it was something Goode did that tipped you off. And Goode went down toward the pool."

"Goode?" Pam repeated. "Oh—Goode! But Jerry, he's just—what's the thing that makes other things come together?"

"That makes—?" Jerry said. "Oh, a catalyst. A catalytic agent."

"Of course," Pam said. "*Now* will you hurry?"

· 13 ·

Mary Hunter wore a bathing suit which was shorts and a bra, which was white and which she had borrowed from Ann Merle. She had swum the length of the pool and back again just as the light faded and then she had stood irresolute a moment and pulled a light coat around her and had looked toward the house and apparently thought better of it. She sat in one of the canvas chairs which was still warm from the sun and seemed to look at the pool and looked at nothing. And after a few minutes, Joshua Merle came down from the house and stood looking down at her. He looked down at her and said, "Hello, Mary."

"Hello," she said.

"It's a funny party," he said. "Do you want a drink? Or anything?"

She said, "No," still looking at nothing across the pool.

He sat down on the grass beside her. He said, "I'm sorry as hell, Mary. About everything."

"So am I," Mary said. "About Rick. About your father. About everything. About little Mr. Potts."

"Yes," Josh Merle said. "But mostly I'm sorry about us. About me."

"I suppose," Mary Hunter said, "that it sounded reasonable enough. He was your father. You hadn't been around much."

"I'd been to Princeton," Josh said.

160

"Oh, Josh!" the girl said. "Oh, for God's sake."

He laughed a little, without amusement. He said he appreciated her defense. He said there was nothing in it.

"I'm not defending you," the girl said. "Why should I defend you? You're somebody I used to know."

"All right," he said. "I can still be sorry about it. I can still be—oh, what the hell." His voice was suddenly tired.

The girl told him he would get over it. She said he would obviously have to get over it.

"All right," he said. "I let you down. Then I let Jameson down." He laughed shortly. "Let him down hard," he added.

She did not say anything. She looked at nothing across the pool.

"My father," he said after a pause, and now his tone was carefully conversational, "had a lot to answer for."

"Well," she said. "He answered for it. The hard way."

Josh said he didn't know. He said there were harder ways. A good many harder ways.

"All right, Josh," she said. "All right."

"He kicked us around," Josh said. "Probably he enjoyed it. What do you think?"

She said she didn't know.

"I think he had it coming," Josh Merle said. "Looking at it abstractly, as if he weren't my father."

"Josh," she said. "You talk like—" She broke off. She came up in her chair and balanced in it, leaning forward, elbows on knees. She looked at the ground and after a moment she said, "Listen, Josh."

"Listen," she said, "There's something the matter with you. I don't know what—maybe it's conscience. You brood over things—over us, over your father, even over Jamie. Over being—hurt."

"Crippled," Josh said, as if he were supplying quite casually, a missing word. "Lame. Limpy."

"Over being lame," she said. "Call it anything you want to. It's an incident. I'm an incident. Even your father is an incident. Heaven knows, Jamie is an incident."

"Murder is a pretty big incident," Josh Merle said. "Crippling your best friend and changing his whole life is a pretty big incident. You—you were a very big incident. I think incident is a hell of a funny word."

"Look," she said. "You can turn a page—read another chapter. Put on another reel of film. You can do that."

"Can you?" he said.

She twisted her body to look at him. Her bra and shorts were white against her skin. In the dusk, they seemed to have a glow of their own, and her eyes seemed to have a different glow.

"Why not?" she said. "I did."

"Without any trouble?"

"Well," she said, "I did it. Everything's some trouble."

He looked at her and said that some things wouldn't be. She looked back at him and did not pretend not to understand, and shook her head.

"No," she said, "this is a new reel. This is another page."

"Is it?" he said. "What makes you so sure?"

He did not move toward her. But it was as if he had moved.

She leaned back suddenly in the chair. It was as if there had been the strand of a spider's silk between them, and her movement had broken it. Words were inessential, but there were words.

"Because that was yesterday," she said. "That was a long time ago. That was when you didn't come and get me, Josh. That was when you believed—when you were a good boy and believed what papa told you. Don't you remember?"

He did not answer for a moment, and then he stood up before he answered. He stood over her and looked down at her and the tension between them was of a new and different kind. Looking up at him, the girl's eyes widened slowly and she started up.

"No," he said. "If I were you, my dear—"

Then he broke off suddenly and turned toward a figure which came toward them.

"Oh, hello," he said. "Hello, Stan. Looking for Ann?"

"I," Goode said, "am almost always looking for Ann, aren't I? Is she down here? Mrs. North thought she was."

"No," Josh Merle said. There was no tension now. He spoke easily, carelessly. "Anyway, I haven't seen her. Have you, Mary?"

"No," the girl said. "Why don't you sit down somewhere, Mr. Goode? Maybe she's around somewhere."

"Why not?" Stanley Goode said. He sat down on the grass by Mary's chair. He looked up at Josh. "Unless, of course," he said, "this is a private fight."

Josh laughed. He said it wasn't a fight. He said he was going to change and have a swim. He walked toward the bathhouse along the concrete edging of the pool. His footsteps were irregular as he walked, and in the gathering darkness his movements were faintly irregular as he limped.

The change in Pamela North was amazing. Hurrying along behind her, Jerry thought that never—not even in her—had he seen so remarkable a change so quickly made. A few minutes ago she had been deep in a lassitude which could hardly—if, Jerry thought, at all—be distinguished from sleep. Now she was—well, now she was very difficult to keep up with, particularly as it was now quite quickly growing dark. Jerry hurried across the lawn and across the flagged terrace and they burst, it seemed to him, into the living room.

Laurel Burke was deep in a chair; enfolded in a chair. She held a cigarette as if holding a cigarette were an effort; looking at them, she lifted a glass and drank and put it down with a gesture which seemed to assure them that there was a duty, discharged against obstacles. Pam North stopped and it seemed to Jerry that she almost skidded. She looked at Laurel Burke and then she looked around the room. She came back to Laurel Burke.

"Where," Pam said, and her voice was hurried, "where is everybody?"

Laurel Burke was languid.

"Well," she said, "I'm here."

Pam's tone dismissed that.

"Everybody else," she said. "Bill Weigand? Sergeant Mullins? That State policeman—what's his name?"

"Sullivan," Laurel told her. "He's good-looking. They all went."

Pam looked at her and shook her head.

"They couldn't have gone," she said. "They couldn't!"

"I don't know why not," Laurel said. "Anyway, they did. They told the old girl—Mrs. Burnside or whatever it is—that there was nothing more they could do here tonight and that they were going. And they went."

"No," Pam said. "I don't believe they went."

It was, Laurel Burke assured her, all the same to Laurel Burke. Maybe they hadn't gone; maybe Mrs. Burnside—

"Burnwood," Jerry said. "Burnwood."

Maybe the old girl made it up; she didn't know the old girl; maybe the old girl did make things up. Maybe Jamie made it up.

"Jameson told you?" Jerry said. It was queer; he agreed with Pam that it was queer.

"Jamie," Laurel said. "Good old Jamie. He told me."

Laurel Burke had, Jerry decided, had a good deal to drink. The fact that she had had a good deal to drink grew on you. Apparently it grew on Pam, because now she turned and walked away. As Jerry watched her she made a quick circuit of the living room. She found it empty, save for Miss Burke. She started out a door and changed her mind.

"Outside somewhere," she said. "Jerry! Come on. We've got to find Bill!"

The Norths went out the way they had come and Laurel's voice, deep as cotton velvet, followed them. "—back to New York," she said. "And I've got to stay here."

In spite of himself, Jerry paused; in spite of himself he turned a little and said, "Why?"

"I," Laurel said, with dignity, "have got to mind the baby."

Jerry was sure afterward that he wasted only a moment considering this, but when he followed Pam onto the terrace it was no longer clear that he was following Pam. At any rate, Pam had disappeared. He started to call her and then decided not to call her. There was something breathless in this sudden darkness; something secret. Pam's urgency communicated itself to Jerry. The thing to do was to find Bill Weigand, or at any rate Sergeant Mullins. Because surely the Burke girl had misunderstood; surely they were still somewhere at Elmcroft.

* * *

Around the corner of the house, where Pam thought she had detected movement—toward which, sure that Jerry was behind her, she had gone at a run—Pam found nobody. But surely there had been somebody there; somebody heading toward—toward the path leading down to the beach and the beach cottage. Pam started toward the path, still almost running. She ran headlong into a very thick and prickly bush. The bush swayed slightly and Pam North bounced.

That wouldn't do. She would have to have a light. She would have to get a light from the house and go down—she started back around the corner of the house, still moving rapidly. She collided with something, but this was not a bush. This gave and made a surprised sound.

"Really, Mrs. North!" a startled, and slightly breathless, voice said. "Really!"

"I'm sorry," Pam said. "I'm sorry, Mrs. Burnwood. How did you know it was me?"

"I see very well in the dark," Mrs. Burnwood said. "Also I have been outside for some time and my eyes have grown accustomed to it." She paused, reflectively. "It seems to me, my dear, that you are behaving very oddly," Mrs. Burnwood said. "Or do you always?"

"Always," Pam told her, to end discussion. "Have you seen Lieutenant Weigand? Or Mullins, the sergeant?"

"But my dear Mrs. North," Mrs. Burnwood said. "They all went back to town. Almost an hour ago." She paused again and patted herself, rearranging not evident disarray caused by collision. "I assumed, Mrs. North, that you and Mr. North had gone also," she said.

Mrs. Burnwood's voice implied that this had been, on the whole, a pleasant assumption.

"No," Pam said. "We're still here. So is Miss Burke."

"Yes," Mrs. Burnwood said. She sighed deeply. "So is Miss Burke." She sighed again, even more deeply.

"Well," Pam said, "excuse me. I've got to find the lieutenant. I'm sure he can't have gone."

"Really," Mrs. Burnwood said. "Really! He and the other policemen certainly drove off in a car. Of course if you don't—."

"All right," Pam said. "All right. Then they came back. Goodbye!"

She went off, along the terrace. It was strange what had happened to Jerry.

There were voices in the living room and she went in toward the voices and the light.

"It's not going to do you any good," Ann Merle said to Laurel Burke. Ann stood looking down at the other girl. Ann's voice was not angry; it was merely indescribably distant and cold.

"I think it is," Laurel said. "I really think it is."

She seemed rather amused. She sipped her drink.

"I think," she said, "that I will really learn to like scotch—now. Now that I can afford such good scotch."

Pam's heels clicked on the polished floor. They both looked at her.

"He's not here," Laurel Burke said. "I told you that. He went back to town. For God's sake." She looked at Ann Merle. "You tell her," she said. "Tell her that the cops have gone. Back to copping."

She laughed; her laughter giggled.

"Yes," Ann said. "They have gone, Mrs. North—Lieutenant Weigand and the others. Didn't you know?"

"They can't—" Pam began and gave it up. "All right," she said. "They've gone. But I've got to find somebody. Where's—where's your brother, Miss Merle?"

Really, Ann Merle told her, she didn't know. Down by the pool? Out on the lawn—or the terrace? With Jamie? Or with Mary Hunter?

"You don't," Pam said, "know where anybody is? Not *any*body?"

Ann Merle shook her head. She gestured vaguely. Everybody was—around.

There was no help there. Desperately, standing again on the terrace, Pam needed help. She needed Jerry—Bill—somebody certain and assured; somebody who would know what to do.

Because what she had done had been wrong; desperately wrong. That was clear now—that was very clear. From the beginning she had been wrong—wrong in theory and so wrong in action; dangerously wrong in action—perhaps fatally wrong in action. And now that she knew, there was nobody to turn to—nobody to help her undo what she had done. And it had to be undone.

Pam could not stand and look wildly into the darkness. The urgency which drove her drove her to action—to almost any action. There were people she had to find and the directions of search were almost infinite. But if she stood still, failure was final, inevitable. Now any action was better than none.

Pam, not running now—feeling her way—listening—went across the terrace, on which her heels no longer clicked. She went onto the lawn and headed away from the house.

"Here," Jerry said, and he was whispering. "Somewhere along here. But I don't know which way she went. I thought I saw something moving over there, but it was Mrs. Burnwood. Then I went—."

"All right," Bill Weigand said. He was whispering, too. "She's somewhere around—in the dark. She's all right this time, Jerry. I wish one or two others were as—but don't worry about her." He fell silent, but his fingers were on Jerry's arm. That was the way they had met, on the far side of the house when Jerry circled it searching for Pam. Out of the darkness, Bill Weigand's hand had closed on Jerry's arm and at the same time Bill had said, softly but with careful clearness, "It's me, Jerry. Bill. Don't talk."

They had not talked, but they had whispered enough—Bill speaking for Mullins and Sullivan, merely darker patches in the darkness. They had driven away. A mile from the house they had driven into a field. They had walked back only when it was dark, coming over the rise on which the house stood. It had taken a long time to get dark.

"The old game," Bill whispered. "Let them think it's a set-up. Walk in on them. Catch them at it."

"At murder?" Jerry said.

Bill Weigand hoped not. But if it were, it wouldn't come off. He spoke with assurance.

"It sure as hell better not come off," Sullivan said, out of the darkness.

"It won't," Bill said. His voice sounded confident. But Jerry, who knew it, had heard it sound more confident. "After all," he said, "it isn't as if we didn't know—it isn't—."

He broke off, listening. They all listened, in the quiet night. But now the night was completely quiet.

"The pool, I think," Bill said. "Somebody splashed—dived, probably. That's the likeliest, anyway. We'll take—." He broke off again and started afresh. "Jerry," he said, "you and I will take a look at the pool. Captain—suppose you have a look at the beach cottage. Mullins—see if you can get in the house and have a look. You know who you're looking for."

"Yeah," Mullins said. "O.K., Loot." He considered. "It don't look to me like we got so much," he said. Thereupon he vanished. After a moment, the solidified darkness which had been Captain Sullivan was also the more rarefied darkness which was merely night. Jerry and Bill Weigand left the terrace where they had been standing and started across the grass.

There was no use in pretending that Stanley Goode was an ideal companion for a girl in a sketchy bathing suit, reclining deep in a deck chair with the night warm all around and fragrant. Mr. Goode was not, at any rate, the ideal companion for Mary Hunter. He was polite, but he was abstracted. No, he hadn't been playing much tennis lately. Yes, he thought he would play a bit later. No, it didn't look like much of a season with so many men in the service. Yes, he—

He stood up.

"I'm sorry, Mrs. Hunter," he said. "I've got to find Ann. If you'll excuse me?"

Whether she would or not—before she had had a chance to—he was gone. He swung off to the left, circling toward the house—hoping, it was clear, to find Ann Merle in some place they knew of; eager to find her anywhere. Mary leaned back and drew the coat around her and looked at nothing across the pool. In a moment, Josh Merle's long body would arch into the pool, diving as he had dived so often during those few weeks of another summer, cutting the water as he had cut it then.

She did not, she told herself, want to see Josh Merle do remembered things, because it brought back the memory of other things—of the failure of his trust in her, of the long, long weeks she had waited for him to come, of the deep hurt. Those things came back too clearly; they seemed to wipe out the interval between—the interval which Rick had made bright. The sight of Josh Merle arching into the pool would bring back memories older than any of her memories of Rick. And that realization was a slow, frightening pain.

She did not go and escape the memories she feared. She waited, knowing that to see Josh again would hurt, and not being able to move to avert the hurt. She thought of ordinary things—of Stanley Goode and his patient, probably futile, devotion to Ann Merle; of the Norths, who had brought her to Elmcroft for reasons which were not clear at first and had since grown less clear; of the long time it was taking Josh to change and dive. And then she thought, with an odd kind of alarm, of Josh's face and his words the moment before Stanley Goode had come and broken the spell between them. There had been a new force in Josh Merle at that moment; a force which was not part of her memories of the summer—a force that might change a great many things; a force which was curiously frightening.

And then, very surprisingly, she heard his steps coming back, and knew them by the slight irregularity, the faint impediment, which now, she found, was a new way he had of hurting her. Because he had been hurt—

She did not look up when he came up beside her chair. She said: "Did you give the idea up?"

"What idea, Mrs. Hunter?" he said. "I seldom give up an idea, once I have it."

At the voice she turned quickly and said, "Oh."

"I thought—" she said. "I thought you were—."

"Yes," he said. "Of course. I suppose we—walk alike. Now. I don't know where Josh is. I suppose he went back to the house. I saw him going that way, as a matter of fact."

"I don't think so, Mr. Jameson," she said. "He went to change. He was going to have a swim."

"Well," Jameson said, "he went up to the house. I guess he changed his mind. Josh changes his mind easily, you know."

"Does he?" the girl said. "I don't know him very well—now."

"Don't you?" Jameson said. "I thought you did. Because, you see—he's still in love with you. I thought you knew that."

His voice seemed gentle.

"No," she said. "I didn't know that. Is he?"

"Oh, yes," Jameson said. "Oh, yes. It's too bad, in a way."

"Why?" she said. "Why is it too bad?"

"Why," Jameson said, "because you don't feel that way about him. Or do you?"

His voice was still gentle. It was the voice of a man sorry that two friends were at cross purposes. It invited confidence. And it was that invitation which made the hesitation evident in Mary Hunter's voice. She said, "No," but her voice hesitated on the word.

Weldon Jameson waited a rather long moment before he answered. When he did speak his voice had a note in it that, at first, Mary Hunter could not understand. But what he said, although not what she expected, was in itself quite simple.

"I wish I could believe that, Mrs. Hunter," Jameson said. "I really wish I could believe that. But I'm really afraid, you know, that you feel about poor Josh just as he feels about you."

Pamela North was more than halfway to the pool when she heard the sound. It was a harmless sound. It was the sound of water splashed suddenly, and the splash had obviously been made by someone diving into the pool—someone swimming on a warm June night. There was nothing frightening in it; nothing to make Pam North's breath catch in her throat or to change her quick walk suddenly into a desperate run. Afterward, Pam was not able to explain to herself why the sound had frightened her, and in the end she admitted that, as she felt then, probably any sound would have frightened her. But at that moment, she did not stop to think about it, but only ran through the darkness, on the yielding turf, downhill a little.

She ran toward the sound. In the darkness near her, someone else was running toward the sound—running more heavily than she was, and running faster. Instinctively, she sheered away from the other runner. The splashing repeated itself in the pool, and now it was more than the sound of someone swimming on a warm June night. It was a thrashing noise, as if more than one person were—

Then, without any warning at all, Pamela North crashed with all the force her slender, pushing legs could give her into something which was hard at first, and then yielded a little and then said something which sounded like "Uh!" with some of the overtones of "oof!" Then the obstacle gave entirely and Pam pitched over it and landed partly on her outstretched hands and partly on less ready portions of her anatomy. She landed on the grass and skidded on hands and knees and then, impetus not being entirely spent, she rolled head over heels and stopped in an odd and, she hurriedly thought, revealing tangle of arms and legs.

She was rolling herself into a ball and shaking her head to clear the surprise out of it, when suddenly lights over the pool went on glaringly. She was on her feet at what she saw in the pool and had started to scream a warning—although clearly things were past the stage of warning—when Jerry came to his feet behind her and Jerry's hands closed on her shoulders.

"Jerry," she said, "I ran into you! Look!"

"Yes," Jerry said. "I was looking for you—thank God!"

The last came because now Bill Weigand and Sergeant Mullins were running toward the pool, and toward the two struggling in it—struggling now in the full glare of floodlights—mercilessly transfixed by the light.

The two were at the deep end of the pool and close to the tiled wall of the pool. The man was clothed and his shirt clung to him and the girl did not seem to be clothed at all. They were struggling together in a kind of desperate confusion. The man had an arm around the girl and was swimming with the other, and even as they watched he seemed to dive, carrying the girl under with him. Then he came up again, and he was pulling—or pushing—at something in the water. And then—only then—he seemed to become conscious of the light and he turned a strange, distorted face toward them.

The girl did not come up. The man dived again as they watched and then—and still Weigand and Mullins were running toward the pool, from toward the end more distant from the struggle in the water—another man appeared out of nowhere and ran across the narrow strip of grass between bathhouse and pool and, without pausing, threw himself into the water. He threw himself on top of the other man and both disappeared.

It had taken seconds—seconds during which a scream hung in Pam North's throat, Jerry's hands gripped hard on her shoulders, Bill Weigand and Mullins ran as if they were running, at slow motion, through quicksand. But actually they were running rapidly, and they seemed to run off the edge of the pool into the water and then—half swimming, half walking with the pressure of the water against them, they went toward the deep end. In seconds more they were both swimming.

But they were still in the middle of the pool when one of the men—it was impossible to see which one, with only the back of a head, dark against the water, to go by—broke water. He looked around wildly; he threw up one hand in what might have been a beckoning gesture—a desperately beckoning gesture—and arched himself into another dive.

Then, out of the turbulence of churning water, he came up again and now he had the girl in his arms, and they could tell it was the girl by her slightness in his arms as he clutched for the pool rim and hooked a hand over it and began to lift her out. The Norths were running by then; they were almost at the pool when Mary Hunter was lifted clear and lay for a moment motionless beside the pool, wearing now only the white shorts of her bathing suit. Pam was already pulling off the light coat she was wearing as she ran toward the still figure, very fragile, helplessly at the mercy of anyone and anything.

Jerry ran with her, but did not try to pass her, and so she reached the pool first. Pam's coat was swinging free by then. She reached the girl just as the man who had thrust her up to the tiles beside the pool started to swing up beside her. Pam took one look at him, swung the coat as if it were a club and engulfed his head in it. Off balance, he made an odd sound and fell over backward into the water.

Pam was kneeling beside the girl and had spread the coat, no longer a weapon, over her when Jerry knelt beside them. But already Pam had the answer for them. Mary Hunter was alive—with a dark bruise on her forehead, with a good deal of water in her, but alive. Pam was about to give artificial respiration, as well as she remembered it, when Jerry stopped her.

"She'll be all right," he said. "But why on earth—?"

He motioned toward the man who, in swimming trunks and with an expression of great anxiety on his face, was swinging up beside them out of the water. He reached toward Mary Hunter and Pam cried out, "Stop him, Jerry!"

But then she stopped, because Mary Hunter opened her eyes and looked up at them, but saw only one of them. She stretched slim bare arms toward him, and Pam, still not understanding what had happened, but conscious that there was a terrible mistake somewhere, and that it was evidently hers, simply knelt and looked at them.

"Josh," the girl said, and although her voice was faint and choked a little, there was a note almost of exultation in it. "Josh—you *did* come back!"

Joshua Merle took the girl, and Pam's coat with her, into his arms and lifted her up against his chest and held her there, his face bent to hers. It seemed to Pam, who was for a moment very near them, that both of them were crying. But they were both so wet that it was, obviously, hard to tell.

Pam stood up then and looked at them, and then looked at Jerry and then spoke.

"Who," Pam North said, "is trying to kill whom?"

She seemed entirely bewildered. Jerry put his arms around her to lessen her bewilderment and they stood watching Weigand and Mullins, who were apparently playing porpoise—diving under the surface, coming up, diving again. But it was on only his second dive that Weigand came up, a little slowly, with the limp body of a man whose thin white shirt was plastered to him.

And then Pam gasped and turned to Jerry, still in his arms, and said: "Jerry! It was the *other* man who limped. It wasn't Josh at all."

Jerry watched Bill Weigand and Mullins lift Weldon Jameson out of the pool, and noticed that Mullins kept his hands on him until Bill had swung out onto the tiles, and kneeling beside the very limp, but, it was now evident, very murderous young man. They were taking no chances, Jerry thought.

"Who limped?" he repeated, then. "Of course they limped—they both limped."

"Behind me," Pam said. "In the cottage—the one who killed Mr. Potts. That was what I remembered that I had forgotten. Before he hit me, I heard him walking behind me. Just a step or two, but there was something wrong with it. Something out of order. And when I heard Stanley Goode walking I knew what it was, because he didn't."

"Didn't?" Jerry said.

Pam was watching Mullins swing up beside Weigand. They began to give Jameson artificial respiration, very expertly. It seemed, Pam thought, rather a cruel thing to do, under the circumstances, but she supposed they had to.

"Didn't what?" Jerry said, because he disliked things left unfinished rather than because he did not already know.

"What?" Pam said. "Oh—limp, of course. Mr. Goode doesn't limp. So naturally I remembered that the man who came up behind me, and hit me on the head, *did* limp. So I thought of course it was Josh Merle, because I never considered Jameson at all, naturally."

"Naturally," Jerry said. He held her closer. He told her, in her ear and only for her, that she was really a very special person. This did not seem to surprise Pam North in the least. But she pressed closer to Jerry and looked up at him, and her face still was puzzled.

"Why?" Pam said. "That's what I don't see—why?"

• 14 •

Laurel Burke was white and tired-looking when she came out of the study with Weigand and Mullins. She looked like a young woman who has been questioned for more than two hours by very expert questioners. Weigand looked tired also—almost as tired as she. Neither he nor the girl nor Mullins spoke as they came out into the living room where the others waited, the French doors to the terrace closed now. Bill crossed to the table of bottles and glasses, indoors now, and mixed two drinks. He gave one to Laurel Burke and drank rather deeply of the other. Mullins mixed rye with water and stood drinking it beside the chair Laurel Burke had chosen. He might have been guarding her.

There was a rather long pause, during which Bill Weigand took another drink from his glass and, after consultation with himself, a third. Then he spoke.

"Miss Burke has been telling us some things," he said. "Haven't you, Miss Burke?"

Laurel Burke merely looked at him.

Bill Weigand did not act as if he had expected her to answer, although he seemed to pause for her answer. When he began again he seemed to begin all over again.

175

"There were two plots against Mr. Merle," he said. "One was against his money. The other was against his life. Miss Burke was in only one of them. She didn't know about the other. Weldon Jameson knew about Miss Burke's little plan—Miss Burke's and Oscar Murdock's. He used what he knew when he decided to kill George Merle."

Bill drank again. When he spoke next he spoke to Joshua Merle, sitting beside Mary Hunter on a sofa.

"Behind everything Jameson did," Bill said, "was an emotion which is in itself very admirable. Behind all of it was loyalty. Not his to you, Mr. Merle—not his to anybody. Your loyalty to him. Your sense of indebtedness to him. You know why you felt it, to the extent you did—to the rather extreme extent you did. Why was it?"

"I've told you," Josh Merle said. "I—." He paused because Mary Hunter's hand had tightened on his. His tone changed. When he spoke again it was slowly, as if he were for the first time examining his attitude toward Jameson.

"It was my fault we cracked up," he said. "Jamie hadn't had much—only his wanting to fly and the chance to fly. He planned to fly after the war—it was all he wanted to do. I banged him up so he'll never get a chance to fly." He broke off. Weigand shook his head in answer to the unspoken thought.

"No," Bill Weigand said, rather grimly. "He won't get a chance to fly. Not now, anyway."

"It was my fault we cracked up," Merle repeated. "I—got flustered or something. I did the wrong thing. There was no excuse for it. Jamie knew there was no excuse for it. We both knew I had to make it up to him."

"Did he say so?" Bill wanted to know.

Merle shook his head.

"Not in words," he said. "He didn't need to. I owed it to him. At least—I felt I did. I—I'm not sure, now, that it made much sense. I admit I took it pretty hard—at any rate I think now that I took it pretty hard. You see—Jamie wasn't the first person I'd—let down."

He looked at Mary Hunter suddenly. She smiled at him.

"I was hipped on the subject," Joshua Merle said, as if he had just realized it. "That was it—I was hipped on the subject of not letting anybody else down."

"Right," Bill Weigand said. "Now—two other things. Your father made you an allowance after you got out of the Navy. It wasn't large. Right?"

"Yes," Merle said.

"The other thing," Bill said. "How did your father feel about Jameson? Did he share your conviction that you would have to go on all your life paying a debt to him? To put it bluntly—taking care of him?"

"No," Merle said. "Dad didn't feel about it the way I did."

Bill Weigand smiled slightly at the understatement; Merle's tone, not by Merle's intention, betrayed how much of an understatement it was.

"You inherit what your father left, Mr. Merle?"

Weigand's words had the form of a statement; they had the inflection of a question.

"Ann and I," he said. "There's enough for both, I guess."

"Right," Weigand said. "So we have a motive."

Pam North, sitting beside Jerry, said, "Oh." Then she said, "Of course!"

"Mr. Jameson killed Mr. Merle so Joshua would have more money," Pam said, explaining aloud to herself. "And then he would get it from Josh."

"Right," Weigand said. "He killed for money, precisely as if he had been going to inherit himself. Because, as long as Joshua Merle kept on feeling the way he did, *wasn't influenced to feel differently,* Jameson was fixed. He hoped he would be fixed for life. And that, Mrs. Hunter, is the reason he tried to kill you. He did try to kill you?"

"He pulled me up and hit me with his fist," Mary said. "The next thing I knew we were both in the water and he was trying to bang my head against the side of the pool."

"The idea being," Bill Weigand said, "that you had slipped and fallen in and that he was trying to save you. But he failed to save you—probably because you had a fractured skull. It would have been hard to prove it was murder, because it was all going to happen in the dark. And even as it was, there wasn't much margin. Mullins and I might have been a little late. Our timing wasn't as good as Mr. Merle's, I'm afraid. To be perfectly honest, it hadn't occurred to me he would turn on you."

"Why did he?" Josh Merle asked. His voice was puzzled.

"Because," Bill said, "he thought that there was a good chance that you and Mrs. Hunter might get married, and that she would convince you that your debt to Jameson was—well, was merely something in your mind. Because—"

"All right," Merle said. He flushed slightly.

"Jamie was perfectly right," Mary Hunter said, not flushing at all. "I thought Josh was all muddled about it. And Jamie did try to find out if Josh and I were—are—" This time she did flush.

"Right," Bill said. "Mr. Jameson saw things going on around him. Not as clearly as Mr. Potts, perhaps—but clearly enough. You threatened the future he had murdered to arrange, Mrs. Hunter. So he decided he might as well kill you, too."

"But—" Pam said. "Like that? Just—casually. He's horrible. Even as murderers go."

Bill Weigand nodded.

"He is," he said. "He is, in an unobtrusive way, as vicious a young man as I ever met. He sent you a message, by the way, Mrs. Hunter. He said he was damned sorry it didn't come off. He seemed to feel he should have planned it better. He said: 'The trouble is, Lieutenant, that I got hurried toward the end.' He said it precisely as if he were explaining why—oh, why he missed a putt."

"Is he talking?" Jerry North asked.

Bill Weigand shook his head. Jameson wasn't talking—for the record. He had sent his message when he and Weigand were alone, before he was locked up. He had also said he would deny ever having sent it; he had said that he would, of course, deny everything, from the murder of George Merle on.

"Then," Pam said, "will you be able to prove it, Bill?"

Bill smiled at her. The smile was tired. He said they could make a case. He said it would be a true case. He said that a jury would have to decide what they had proved. He was non-committal. But when Pam looked at him with special intensity, he nodded just perceptibly. Pam decided he was pretty sure what the jury would decide.

"So—" Weigand said. "I am using you all as a jury, in a way. As jury and witnesses both. We have a motive for the murder of your father, Mr. Merle—and for the attack on Mrs. Hunter. By the way, Mrs. Hunter, did he say anything to you—ask anything—about your—your attitude toward Mr. Merle?"

The girl did not reply. She looked at Josh Merle for a moment and half smiled. She looked at Bill Weigand. Then she nodded.

She would probably have to testify to that, Bill Weigand told her. If they could get it in. It would be pretty far afield, but maybe they could get it in.

"Now, Mr. Merle," Bill said. "You had an appointment to meet Mr. Jameson at Charles yesterday evening?" He looked at his watch and saw it was after midnight. "Tuesday evening," he said.

Merle nodded.

"Did you, as far as you remember, tell anyone else about it?" Bill asked.

Merle thought and then shook his head. Then he thought of something and spoke.

"But," he said, "it wasn't Jamie who called me up." He spoke with confidence, but then he looked puzzled. "I don't think it was," he said.

Bill smiled faintly. He said that this was a difficulty. He had thought it would be. He said the defense was going to make a lot of that.

"I'm convinced that it was," he said. "It had to be—and Jameson lied about it. That was the discrepancy. That was what really convinced me that he was the man we wanted. Because, you see, he made it clear that he had just happened to be walking toward Charles when he ran into you. But you, Mr. Merle, said that you had decided not to wait for Jamie after you got the telephone call and had run into him outside as he was coming in. Remember?"

"Well," Josh Merle said, "that was the way it was. But how—?"

"From the drug store on the corner," Bill told him. "It's only a few feet down the street. I think he called you from there, came out quickly and walked toward the restaurant, being pretty certain he would pick you up. As he did. We're trying to find somebody in the drug store who can identify him; we have been all evening. If we can, we've got him. Because—" he broke off and smiled slightly—"Because, ladies and gentlemen of the jury, *that call was made to Mr. Merle by somebody who knew his father had been killed. And at that time, nobody knew it but the police, Mrs. Hunter and Mr. and Mrs. North.* The police didn't call; the Norths and Mrs. Hunter didn't call. The murderer called. Jameson called. He disguised his voice. I think you'll decide, Mr. Merle, that you can't swear it *wasn't* Jameson. That you can't swear either way."

"But why?" Mrs. North said. "Why did he call at all?"

Because, Bill Weigand told her, he wanted to be in on the investigation. He wanted to be where he could watch it—where he could do whatever the turn of the investigation indicated. And the only way he had to do that was to go along with Joshua Merle, who would naturally be questioned. He wanted to be in from the start; he therefore arranged that Merle should be in from the start.

Pam said, "Oh." She said, "Did he—" and stopped, her eyes wide.

"Precisely," Bill said. "He found that we suspected Murdock. For good reason. So he gave us Murdock—on a marble slab. Murdock, confessing by suicide that he had killed Mr. Merle. Ending the case by his suicide—except that he had a broken wrist which was improperly set. And that you noticed it, Pam."

"You mean—he killed Murdock just for that?" Jerry North asked.

"Right," Weigand said. He seemed surprised at the doubt in Jerry's tone. "What better motive? He didn't care who he killed—you'd have to talk to him to realize how little he cared. And, if it worked, killing Murdock so as to suggest suicide would bring the whole case to an end—with Mr. Jameson comfortably in the clear. It was a very reasonable murder, Murdock's was. As a matter of fact, Jameson is a very reasonable murderer. He is quite unhampered by emotions. He killed only when it could reasonably be expected to do him some good."

"But," Pam said, "Mr. Potts?"

Bill shrugged. That, precisely, they would never know, he said. If it came into the trial they would merely have to suggest that Mr. Potts had discovered something—something tangible—that pointed to Jameson as the murderer and that Jameson had discovered that Mr. Potts knew something.

"But," he said, "I don't think that Mr. Potts had discovered anything tangible. Probably Jameson thought he had. Or perhaps Jameson thought he would find something—or put us in the way of finding something. I think that Potts was killed purely and simply because he was too observant—because he, of all those who knew Jameson, really knew him—really knew that if murder was being done and Jameson were around, Jameson was the man to watch. Because of the kind of man he was. I don't think Mr. Potts knew any more than that."

He paused.

"Nothing tangible," he said. "Only observation and reason—only the faculties of the human mind, developed beyond the average. Mr. Potts was a very intelligent man. I think that that cost him his life. We'll never know, but that is what I think. Mr. Potts went beyond facts to the truth once too often."

He finished his drink and poured another. The rest waited. Bill Weigand sat down with this drink and still they waited.

"Now," he said finally, "we come to the beginning. Which is where Miss Burke and Murdock came in." He looked at Miss Burke. "Miss Burke has decided not to press her point about the child," he said, dryly. "Haven't you, Laurel?"

Laurel Burke looked at him with quiet hate. He waited.

"To hell with you," she said. "All right."

"Because," he said, "if Miss Burke doesn't bother you, and if she testifies as we expect her to, we won't bother Miss Burke. About the plan she and Mr. Murdock had to collect from Mr. Merle."

He hesitated. He said that part of this was rather embarrassing, because it did not throw an entirely pleasant light on George Merle.

"All right," Mrs. Burnwood said, unexpectedly and brusquely. "All right. We all know George wasn't a saint."

He hadn't been, Weigand agreed. He told the story without emotion, explaining that he was summarizing what Laurel Burke had told him.

They must understand, to begin with, that Oscar Murdock had done a good many odd chores for George Merle. Some had to do with business; some had not. Among the latter was—Weigand paused for an inoffensive word—making preliminary arrangements with attractive young women from time to time. They need not go into that, except that Laurel Burke was one of the young women—the last of the young women. Mr. Murdock had made preliminary arrangements after Mr. Merle, who had heard her singing in a small night club, had expressed interest. The preliminary arrangements completed satisfactorily, Murdock had made further arrangements, because Mr. Merle had found in Miss Burke something he had been looking for, for some time.

"Mr. Merle was a careful man," Weigand pointed out. "He was anxious not to jeopardize his position. Murdock had no position. So ostensibly, Murdock and Laurel set up housekeeping on Madison Avenue. Mr. Merle planned to use it as a cover; for a while he did."

But Mr. Merle had placed more trust in Murdock than Murdock deserved. Murdock saw a chance to improve on the situation and Miss Burke agreed to the improvements.

"One of which," Weigand said, "was that Laurel and Murdock made their ostensible relationship their real relationship."

Weigand paused and thought that over. He apparently concluded that there was no more delicate way of saying it.

They also decided that the surest hold a young woman on the make could have on a rich man who was paying her rent was to have a child by him.

"But she didn't," Weigand said. "She decided she wasn't going to. So Murdock—coöperated."

Laurel Burke swore at him suddenly and uglily.

"Miss Burke," Bill said, undisturbed, "prefers the theory that she and Murdock fell in love. In either event, the results were—as planned. Miss Burke is really going to have a baby. Presumably Murdock's in fact; certainly Mr. Merle's according to the story she and Murdock told Mr. Merle."

Murdock pretended, of course, that he was still a faithful employee of Merle. He remained, in Merle's eyes, merely an arranger. When

Laurel began to demand money in view of her condition—and to talk of a large lump sum settlement—Murdock pretended that he was only the messenger who carried her demands, although in fact he was the one who, with his knowledge of how far Merle could be driven, fixed the amount of the demands. Everything went according to their plan. As part of the plan, Laurel left the apartment on Madison Avenue and went into "hiding"—partly merely to. worry Merle; chiefly, Weigand thought, to keep Merle from going directly to Laurel.

"Murdock thought he had better keep it all in his own hands," Weigand explained. "Probably because he didn't fully trust Miss Burke."

He looked at Laurel Burke. She had closed her eyes and said nothing.

"Incidentally," Weigand said, "Murdock decided to sublet the apartment, not being a man to waste if waste could be avoided. It was chance—but not a long chance, since he knew her—that led him to rent it to Mrs. Hunter. He told nobody—not Laurel nor Jameson."

"Jameson?" Josh Merle repeated. "Did he know about it?"

Weigand nodded. After a certain stage he had.

They could assume that for some time Jameson had realized that George Merle was an obstacle to his plan of living on Joshua Merle for the rest of his life. They could assume that he had already been an obstacle; that Jameson's presence was one of the reasons George Merle kept his son's allowance low. Jameson had looked around for something to do about it, no doubt at first something short of murder. Luck played into his hands when he happened to see George Merle and Laurel together at the Zero Club which, because it was out of the way in a good many respects, Merle considered safe.

Jameson thought he might make something out of that and investigated. He suspected Murdock was in it, knowing that Murdock was usually in things, and—half by persuasion and half by veiled threats— got Murdock to introduce him to Laurel Burke.

Out of Laurel he got the whole story because—

"He guessed part of it," Laurel Burke interrupted, her voice tired and no longer carefully husky. "He was a smart one—he figured part of it out. Somehow he guessed that Ozzie and I were—were keeping house. He made me think he would go to old man Merle unless we came through with the story. But he didn't want to be cut in and—hell, he was on the make too. He was just one of the crowd. So, one time and another, I told him most of it."

She stopped and lay back in the chair, her eyes closed. She had, apparently, made her contribution.

"Jameson didn't want to be cut in because he got another idea," Weigand said. "He decided to use Laurel and Murdock as a cover. If Merle died suddenly, particularly in the Madison Avenue apartment, the Laurel-Murdock angle would come out. And they would be mixed up in it—if it was murder. Particularly if he planted a few clues for the police that mixed them up in it. Once the police found out what Murdock and Laurel were up to, they wouldn't—Jameson figured—bother to look any further."

It had seemed like a good opportunity, with suspects ready-made. So Jameson, finding out the stage of the negotiations for collecting from Merle, wrote a letter inviting Merle to come to the Madison Avenue apartment to pay off. He set the amount of the payoff low as an inducement and Merle, having no reason to suspect anything but the shakedown he was expecting, went with a check in his pocket. Jameson presumably had suggested a check because a demand for cash might make Merle cautious—might even lead him to bring a bodyguard along. Probably Jameson rather hoped that the check would be made out to cash, in which case he could regard it as a bonus.

He got into the apartment ahead of Merle—they would have to find out how, but presumably by walking up from the ground floor and using a skeleton key in the old lock. They were working on that. When Merle came, Jameson let him in and shot him. He took the check, found it was made out to Murdock—Murdock had arranged that method of payment, persuading Merle that it would leave less open trace than a check made out to cash—and sent it by mail to the bank for deposit to Murdock's account. He hoped this would lead the police to believe that Murdock had been there and got the check himself. He left the letter he had written Merle and signed with Murdock's initials—and had written, it appeared, with gloves on, so that only Merle's fingerprints would show. He left the apartment, walking down the stairs and avoiding the elevator man, and took a cab at Sixth Avenue and made his call to Joshua Merle.

"After that," Weigand said, "he just did what was necessary as it came up. A lot came up."

Weigand finished his drink and stood up.

"Which," he said, "is that—is all of it. He'll be tried in the city for Merle's murder; he'll be indicted for the other murders and, if it seems advisable, for the attack on Mrs. Hunter. And Mullins and I will be getting along back."

Jerry North stood up and looked at Pamela, and she stood up too.

"Of course," she said. "It's awfully late." She turned to Mrs. Burnwood. "Thank you for having us," she said, and her voice sounded sleepy. "It's been very—" She seemed suddenly to realize what she was saying. "Oh!" Pam North said.

Then she looked at Mary Hunter inquiringly, because Mary had come out with them. Joshua Merle's arm lay along the back of the sofa and Mary Hunter's head was resting on it. Mary's eyes were closed and it did not look as if she had any intention of riding back to New York with the Norths.

"Or," Pam said to herself, "with anybody."

So Pam gave Jerry a little push toward the door and they went out after Bill and Sergeant Mullins.